CONTENTS

A Tale of the Secret Saint

NOVEL

2

WRITTEN BY
Touya

ILLUSTRATED BY
chibi

Airship

Seven Seas Entertainment

Tensei Sita Daiseijyo ha, Seijyo dearuko towohitakakusu Vol.2
© Touya, chibi 2019
Originally published in Japan in 2019
by EARTH STAR Entertainment, Tokyo.
English translation rights arranged
with EARTH STAR Entertainment, Tokyo,
through TOHAN CORPORATION, Tokyo.

Seven Seas press and purchase enquiries can be sent to
Marketing Manager Lianne Sentar at press@gomanga.com.
Information regarding the distribution and purchase of
digital editions is available from Digital Manager CK Russell
at digital@gomanga.com.

Follow Seven Seas Entertainment online at
sevenseasentertainment.com.

TRANSLATION: Kevin Ishizaka
ADAPTATION: Matthew Birkenhauer
COVER DESIGN: H. Qi
LOGO DESIGN: George Panella
INTERIOR LAYOUT & DESIGN: Clay Gardner
COPY EDITOR: Meg van Huygen
PROOFREADER: Jade Gardner
LIGHT NOVEL EDITOR: Rebecca Scoble
PREPRESS TECHNICIAN: Melanie Ujimori
PRINT MANAGER: Rhiannon Rasmussen-Silverstein
PRODUCTION MANAGER: Lissa Pattillo
EDITOR-IN-CHIEF: Julie Davis
ASSOCIATE PUBLISHER: Adam Arnold
PUBLISHER: Jason DeAngelis

ISBN: 978-1-64827-647-7
Printed in Canada
First Printing: April 2022
10 9 8 7 6 5 4 3 2 1

THE STORY THUS FAR

THREE HUNDRED YEARS AGO, the world was full of people called saints—women with the ability to use healing magic. The greatest of them all was known as the Great Saint.

The Great Saint, a princess, used her power for the sake of her people. Although she successfully sealed away the demon lord, her cruel brothers—the princes of the realm—betrayed her, leaving her to an agonizing death.

In the modern era, a hopeful fifteen-year-old girl by the name of Fia Ruud was attacked by the strongest of all monsters: a black dragon. But while on death's door, she remembered that she was the Great Saint in a past life.

She used her newfound healing power to survive and make the black dragon her familiar. Still fearing the demon that put an end to her past life, she decided to hide the fact that she's a saint and live as a knight.

While hiding her saint powers, she breezed through the Knight Brigade admission exam and was assigned to the prestigious First Knight Brigade—but an encounter with a powerful monster caused eyes to fall on her. She displayed knowledge and leadership ability no recruit could possibly have.

First Knight Brigade Captain Cyril then sent her to the Fourth Monster Tamer Knight Brigade to gauge the health of their familiars, but not everything went as planned...

Náv Kingdom
CHARACTER LIST

FIA RUUD

Youngest daughter of the Ruud knight family. A princess and the Great Saint in her past life. Currently hiding her status as a saint and living as a knight...for now.

ZAVILIA

Fia's familiar. The only black dragon in the world. One of the Three Great Beasts of the continent.

SAVIZ NÁV

Commander of the Náv Black Dragon Knights. The younger brother of the king and, as such, the heir apparent.

CYRIL SUTHERLAND

Captain of the First Knight Brigade. Head of the most prominent duke family and second in line to the throne. Also known as the "Dragon of Náv." Strongest swordsman in the entirety of the Knight Brigade.

DESMOND RONAN

Captain of the Second Knight Brigade and Commandant of the Military Police. His family rules an earldom. Also known as the "Tiger of Náv." Has had a grudge against women ever since his younger brother ran off with his fiancée.

QUENTIN AGUTTER

Captain of the Fourth Monster Tamer Knight Brigade. Can judge one's strength through an aura visible to him alone.

ZACKARY TOWNSEND

Captain of the Sixth Knight Brigade. Well liked by his subordinates. Chivalrous and caring.

Náv Black Dragon Knight Brigade
COMMANDER: SAVIZ NÁV

	Captain	Vice-Captain	Knight
First Knight Brigade ROYAL FAMILY GUARDS	Cyril Sutherland		Fia Ruud, Fabian Wyner
Second Knight Brigade ROYAL CASTLE SECURITY	Desmond Ronan		
Third Mage Knight Brigade MAGES	Enoch		
Fourth Monster Tamer Knight Brigade MONSTER TAMERS	Quentin Agutter	Gideon Oakes	Patty
Fifth Knight Brigade ROYAL CAPITAL GUARDS	Clarissa Abernethy		
Sixth Knight Brigade MONSTER EXTERMINATION, ROYAL CASTLE VICINITY	Zackary Townsend		
Seventh Knight Brigade MONSTER EXTERMINATION, NORTH			
Eighth Knight Brigade MONSTER EXTERMINATION, EAST			
Ninth Knight Brigade MONSTER EXTERMINATION, SOUTH			
Tenth Knight Brigade MONSTER EXTERMINATION, WEST			
Eleventh Knight Brigade BORDER PATROL, FAR NORTH			
Twelfth Knight Brigade BORDER PATROL, FAR EAST			
Thirteenth Knight Brigade BORDER PATROL, FAR SOUTH			
Fourteenth Knight Brigade BORDER PATROL, FAR WEST		Dolph Ruud	
Fifteenth Knight Brigade BORDER PATROL			
Sixteenth Knight Brigade BORDER PATROL			
Seventeenth Knight Brigade BORDER PATROL			
Eighteenth Knight Brigade BORDER PATROL			
Nineteenth Knight Brigade BORDER PATROL			
Twentieth Knight Brigade BORDER PATROL			

19

The Fourth Monster Tamer Knight Brigade Part 3

QUENTIN, the man resembling a large and nimble cat, stared at the puppet on my hand without saying a word.

H-huh? Why isn't he saying anything? I wondered before finally remembering Zavilia's words. *Oh, right...explain first, then show.*

I flashed him a friendly smile. "This puppet here actually has a second function! It can be used as outerwear for my Blue Dove familiar when he's cold!"

Silence.

Uhh...maybe he's the quiet type? Then I, uh...probably shouldn't bother him.

"A-anyway..." I said, beginning to back away. "Let me just get out of your hair..."

Right then, Quentin finally spoke. "Splendid! What wonderful craftsmanship! Why, for a moment I even believed the thing was alive. It so clearly reflects the artistic talent of its creator! And I see you are gifted in wordplay as well—am I correct in assuming you chose the 'bluebird of happiness' as a motif for this piece? I must say, the black and blue contrast very well."

I froze, stunned by his sudden rambling. *What is this man on about?* My mind raced as I tried to think up a suitable response.

Before I could say anything, Gideon exclaimed hysterically, "C-Captain, why are you speaking so formally to this low-ranking knight?! And was that supposed to be a puppet? All I see is some gnarled piece of cloth—"

Gideon was suddenly interrupted by a painful-sounding stomp on the foot from Quentin.

Oh, Gideon. Did you learn nothing from Captain Cyril's scolding? That's no way to speak to a lady, nor of her art. You should take a page from Captain Quentin's book and learn to act more like a gentleman, I thought, bobbing my head up and down in approval.

Confused, Cyril gave Quentin a look. "Is something the matter, Quentin? It's not like you to try to flatter someone. Did your long expedition take a toll on you? Is your head feeling all right?"

Quentin shot Cyril a death glare. "Cyril, we need to talk."

He took Cyril over to the corner of the room, grabbed him by the collar, and whispered, "Nobody understands how to handle monsters better than me, so if you value your life, shut it and follow my lead!"

"What are you talking about?" said Cyril. "Wait, you don't seriously think that Blue Dove is some threatening monster, do you? Surely the captain of the Fourth Monster Tamer Knight Brigade wouldn't make that kind of mistake."

"Shut *up*!" Quentin exclaimed. "There's no telling what might set it off, so zip it!"

Cyril, his back pressed against the wall, looked dubiously back at Quentin, but he eventually folded. "All right. I haven't a clue what you're getting at, but I'll play along."

"Ugh." Quentin sighed. "You don't know how good you have it, being so blissfully unaware."

The two returned, and Quentin immediately began heaping praise onto Zavilia. "Please forgive Cyril here. It seems he doesn't understand the magnificence that is your elegant black-and-blue familiar. How one could not recognize such a sublime thing is lost on me."

I looked at Cyril to see his usual smile gone, a look of complete confusion in its place.

Don't worry, Captain. I don't have a clue what's going on either!

Quentin plastered on a smile and beckoned toward the sofa. "You must be tired from standing. Please, have a seat."

But then his gaze traveled down to the sofa, and he saw the smashed table, which made him jump. "Wh-what?! Who did this? Was it you, Cyril?!"

Cyril frowned. "What makes you think that I did it, hmm? I see no reason you should cast doubt on me. Even supposing I *did* break the table, I'd still be offended by the sudden accusation."

"This table is made from black ironwood! There's no way Gideon or Patty could break it, so who else could...it...be..." Quentin grew quiet, as though a sudden truth had dawned on

him. He turned around with a shocked look on his face. "Was it...
you, perchance?"

"Huh?" *M-me? I'm just some weak recruit. There's no way I
could've broken it!*

He seemed to have misunderstood something as he fixed up
an awkward smile. "*Ohhh*, so it was you after all! In that case, I
have nothing but gratitude. I'd been thinking this table was much
too big and would be just perfect if it were split in half. Thank
you so very much."

Cyril's frown deepened. "Did you eat something spoiled?
You've been speaking nonsense for a while now."

"You'd do well to hold your tongue, Sir Cyril!" Quentin
snapped. "Just follow along with what I say, if you value your
life!"

"Why are you trying to speak so formally? You're clearly no
good at it," Cyril said with a sigh. "Look, I know I said I'd play
along, but I'm no longer sure what we're even *playing* at."

"Of course you're not," said Quentin. "Not even I know if I'm
on the right track."

"Completely incoherent," Cyril muttered. "The long expedition must've really done a number on your head..."

Huh... I looked at the two captains with concern. *It's nice
they're such good friends, but how much longer are they going to
keep up whatever...this is? I need to go meet Charlotte soon, like I
promised.*

Noticing my look of concern, Cyril questioned me. "What's
wrong, Fia?"

"Uh, well, I promised to meet up with Charlotte soon. I was thinking maybe I could take my leave? If that's all right?"

"Who's Charlotte? A knight from this brigade?" Cyril asked.

"No, she's a saint living in the Royal Castle. We're supposed to feed healing potion to the familiars together today," I answered.

Cyril seemed at a loss for words for a moment. "This saint...allows you to call her by name? She even promised to meet with you?"

"Uhh, yep. She's really lonely from living away from her family, so I'm temping as a mom," I answered, fondly remembering that time Charlotte had even asked me to call her by name.

Cyril's expression soured. "Mother? I don't know how old Her Grace is, but she can't be much younger than ten. Unless you're telling me you could conceive at five years old, I'm pretty sure calling yourself her older sister is more apt—that is, assuming she *is* as fond of you as you say. Either way, I'd feel more at ease if you acted as her older sister instead. Just imagining how *you* might raise an impressionable young saint frightens me."

I giggled at the joke. "Nice one, Captain Cyril! As if anything could frighten the proud captain of the First Knight Brigade." But wait—I'd almost forgotten something important. "Oh, right! Captain Cyril, allow me to introduce you to my cute little familiar, Zavilia. He's only zero years old, so I'm basically his mother—more mother than before, anyway!" I stroked Zavilia's head. He narrowed his eyes and purred happily.

"M-M-Miss Fia, wouldn't it be more appropriate to refer to your familiar by the first letter of its name?" Quentin asked nervously.

"Huh?" I blurted. *Oh...come to think of it, Patty did mention something like that. But I thought it was okay for a familiar's master to call them by name?*

"I-If you call your familiar directly by name, others around you might hear and do the same. And, well...we wouldn't want anyone to make such a blunder, would we?" Quentin pushed back his hair, let out an odd, jangling sort of laugh, and continued. "Familiars dislike it when someone other than their master utters their name, so everyone in our brigade refers to them by letter. Oh, b-but, of course, if your familiar is proud of their name and would take offense to it being reduced to a letter, I completely understand! But if that's the case, you should never—under any circumstances *whatsoever*—say their name around others." He put a lot of emphasis into his words, insisting more than recommending.

He sure knows his stuff. I guess he wasn't captain of the Fourth Monster Tamer Knight Brigade for nothing! "Oh, I see," I said with a nod. "That makes sense."

That was when Gideon chimed in with a rather rude outburst. "Captain, you don't need to bother teaching our rules to this brat! She just lucked out on finding a familiar that was already half-dead! It's a runty little thing anyway. What's it going to do if we call it by name? Peck us? What're ya going to do, Zav—*koff!*"

Gideon was abruptly interrupted by Quentin again—with a flying knee to the abdomen. "C-Captain...why?" He looked up at Quentin from the ground, his face a mixture of pain and confusion.

Quentin looked down on him with cold eyes. "How dull are you people?!" he bellowed. "If you know what's good for you, you'll all keep your traps shut!"

Why's he yelling? I wondered. *Maybe he's grumpy because he's hungry?*

Weird as he was acting, I still had to move on. I made my way to the door and put my hand on the handle. "Everyone seems busy," I said quietly, "so I think I'll go... Captain Cyril, thank you for checking on me. I'll report in when I finally make some progress. Patty, I'll inform you of any new developments regarding the healing potion feeding. Captain Quintin, you seem exhausted. I recommend you eat till you're full and get a good night's sleep. Vice-Captain Gideon, you'll get a sore back if you sleep on the floor." I spoke louder again—"And with that, I shall take my leave!"—and quickly dashed out, shutting the door before anyone could stop me. I let out a big sigh of relief as I leaned against the closed door.

Phew...that was close. Any longer and I'd be making Charlotte wait.

With Zavilia on my shoulder, I scurried down the hallway. Still, Quentin's advice bothered me... "Hey, Zavilia. Do you want me to call you by your first letter, like Quentin said?"

"You can call me what you like. However, I've gone a long time without anyone calling me by name, so I think I'd prefer my full name."

I smiled. "Then let's stick with Zavilia!"

Together, we made our way to the familiar stables.

Charlotte was already there waiting for me, so I ran right up to her. "Charlotte! Sorry I made you wait!"

She smiled back at me. "It's okay. Waiting wasn't bad, 'cause I knew for sure you'd come. Meeting with friends like this is nice, isn't it?"

"Agh, so *cute*! Aww, Charlotte! I swear, I'll become the best older sister ever for you!" I covered my mouth with both hands, absolutely taken by this cute, blushing girl.

But what was she holding? A jar of green liquid was clutched against her chest. "Oh! Charlotte, did you collect some healing potion from the spring? Thank you!"

She smiled back brightly, giving me the sudden urge to please her even more. So I took out my puppet and put it on my left hand.

"Nice to meet you, Charlotte! My name is Zav..." I stopped, remembering how Quentin warned against saying Zavilia's name in front of others. "My name is Zabby! Zabby likes apples. He's a bluebird-type monster! Zabby says happiness is coming your way! So smile, okay?"

I put effort into moving the puppet, even using my right hand, but Charlotte's smile looked more than a little awkward. Even Zavilia's expression was tolerant at best—he seemed to hate it.

H-huh? Th-they don't like it? L-let's just stop... I was smart enough to know when to stop digging my own grave.

We all pretended like I hadn't just embarrassed myself and entered the familiar stables. As we walked, Charlotte eagerly told me about the familiars and what she'd learned from previous visits. But her smile grew thinner and thinner the more we checked on the poor injured familiars. Four checkups later, it might've never been there at all. She came to a stop and clutched at my uniform.

"Charlotte? Is something wrong?"

"Their injuries are... They're *gone*..."

"Well, yeah? We fed them healing potion and they're healed. That simple, right?" Maybe Charlotte still had some doubts about the green healing potion.

"B-but it's too fast! It should take at least a week for them to heal!"

"Green healing potions boost the user's natural recovery, and monsters *already* have a pretty high recovery rate. It's no wonder it only took a day to heal."

She clenched the hem of my uniform with both hands, lips trembling. "Then this green water...this is really healing potion?"

I grinned. "You know it." That was when I noticed the tears starting to fall from her eyes. "Huh? Hey, Charlotte, what's wrong?"

"This healing potion is amazing. It doesn't hurt anyone, it heals so quickly, I...I've been wanting something like this for so long!"

I pulled her in close and patted her back. "That's good, right? Heh. I'm returning to the First Knight Brigade, so make sure to tell everybody in the Fourth Monster Tamers, okay? My captain personally came to check up on me, so I bet it'll be any day now."

Charlotte looked up with a start. "You're leaving?"

"Yep. It's my Brigade, after all. But the First Knight Brigade is stationed in the Royal Castle, so we can still see each other whenever we want." I bent down to her height and smiled. "Can you do one thing for me? The healing water spring you made will get diluted as time goes by and new water comes in. Can you add your healing magic to it every day? And that'll be good practice too. The same amount you used last time is enough. Be careful not to overdo it, or you'll wind up magic fatigued."

She fell into silent thought for a moment before speaking. "Are you...a saint?"

"Ah, uh. Ha, um." I swallowed. "What?"

"I sometimes get lessons from the high-ranking saints. They hold my hand and show me how to let my healing magic flow, but I never learned anything. I'm too talentless." Charlotte looked up at the ceiling thoughtfully. "When you held my hand at the spring, I felt my magic flow for the first time. You even told me to control the magic I was releasing from my left hand. The way you taught me was so different from all the higher-ranking saints, and I wasn't sure at first, but now I've seen what this green healing potion can do. I'm sure of it... You're a saint, and the strongest I've ever seen."

"Oh...Charlotte..."

"It should take more than ten high-ranking saints to turn an entire spring into healing potion. Um." She paused. "Fia? In the church, there's a portrait of the legendary Great Saint. She has beautiful deep-crimson hair and golden eyes...just like you."

I didn't know what to say.

"If people knew you had powerful healing magic," she said, "and you even looked like the Great Saint, you'd be worshipped—enshrined, even."

"Enshrined? That sounds...like a lot." *Yikes, anything but that.* I couldn't stop myself from grimacing. Even my last life gave me more freedom than *that*.

Charlotte looked as though she'd made up her mind about something. "I'll always be on your side, Fia," she said seriously. "I won't do anything you wouldn't want." She took her dainty little hands and wrapped them tightly around mine. "I know you're a wonderful saint because you made that healing potion spring to help the familiars. You even showed me how to use my powers. So if there's a reason you don't want anyone to know, then I won't tell anyone."

She looked straight into my eyes now. "Thank you for making me a saint. I've always wanted to be able to help people, and now I can. Thank you so much..."

Her words put me at ease. "You're very welcome, Charlotte. Congratulations on becoming a fine saint, and thank you for respecting my wishes."

Zavilia interrupted our heart-to-heart moment with a whisper. **"Smart girl. For a moment, I thought I'd need to deal with her."**

Um! That was a little unsettling, but I decided not to comment on it. Everything had been resolved nice and clean, after all. "Shall we go check on the rest of the familiars, Charlotte?" I said cheerfully, trying to brighten the mood.

We went around and checked the remaining injured familiars. I breathed a sigh of relief—almost all of them were completely healed. As we checked the last familiar, Charlotte muttered, "This green healing potion really is amazing... They're all healed, and they're all so friendly too."

Now that she mentioned it, yeah—the monsters that were aggressive toward me yesterday were practically cuddly now.

"It may not seem like much to you," said Charlotte, "but this green healing potion really is amazing. It's nothing like the clear healing potion that everyone uses. It might... Well, it might even be a problem if people find out about it."

"Huh? Why?"

Sure, the pain from using the clear healing potion sucked, but it only caused me all that pain because I could use healing magic. It should be bearable for most people, unless... Wait, no, is she talking about how fast the green healing potion works? When I drank the clear healing potion, I actually used my magic to heal myself...so I don't really know how long those potions take to work. Maybe I should've let the clear stuff run its course to figure that out. Then again, that pain was just awful!

"Hey, Fia?" Charlotte's voice snapped me back to reality right as my train of thought was about to derail. "For now, let's just use this green healing potion for the familiars here. We can just say it looks different because it's for monsters."

"All right, sounds good," I said, a little taken aback. "You're really smart for a child." *Both Zavilia and Charlotte are such smart kids. I really gotta catch up with 'em!*

"You're fine just the way you are, Fia. I suspect that if you got too motivated, it would cause...problems."

Don't be like that, Zavilia! I can do anything if I try!

"Just watch me!" I whispered aloud.

Zavilia just sighed.

Wouldn't you know it, I just happened to cross paths with Quentin right after parting ways with Charlotte.

"Ack! M-Miss Fia!" He must've showered and washed his clothes—his hair was wet, and the damp and tattered knight uniform he'd worn earlier was clean now.

Captain Quentin must've gone and checked on Vice-Captain Gideon first thing, before even freshening up after his trip. What a nice captain!

"Where are you headed, Captain Quentin?" I asked, looking up to meet his eyes.

"W-w-well! I haven't had a decent meal in a while, so I thought I might go to the canteen?"

"Ha! That's fun, I'm headed there too for lunch! Mind if I join you?"

"Wh-what?! J-join...me?" He seemed perplexed. He muttered something quickly under his breath, "This could be a good opportunity to gain valuable information on the black dragon. Nothing ventured, nothing gained, after all. Then again...I suppose refusal isn't even an option, is it?" Then he forced an awkward smile. "It would be an honor to eat with you, Fia."

It was past lunchtime, so the canteen was fairly empty. Still, a good number of knights noticed Quentin and walked up to greet him.

My, my. Somebody's popular. I picked out some food and brought it back, only to find Quentin standing by a table, waiting for me.

"Sorry for making you wait," I said as I sat down. Right on cue, Quentin sat with me. *Whoa, what a gentleman! He waits for the lady to sit first? Impressive!*

Still, was he really going to just have a glass of water for lunch? "I thought you said you were hungry."

"Ha ha! Ha! Haaaa...truthfully, I'm so nervous right now that I don't think I could keep anything down."

"Ohh, I get it. You've got that post-expedition full-body tension! You're just letting it rest until you get back in the swing of things. Is that it?"

"Ha ha ha ha ha...*haaaah*." Empty laughter, followed by an *impressively* long sigh.

Huh. Captain Quentin's a weird one, I guess. Eh, I'll figure him out eventually.

I started digging in when I noticed him sneaking glances at my left wrist...maybe? I couldn't tell for sure, because he kept looking away every time I glanced at him.

I held my left wrist out. "Is something about my wrist bothering you?"

"Huh? Um, do you mind if I look?"

"Uh. Sure, go ahead. There's nothing special about it. *Ohh,* but I do have my proof of pact right there."

He stared intently at my wrist without saying a word, checking both sides of my wrist and even running his finger over my proof of pact.

Oh, I know that look! That's the intense look I get whenever healing magic is involved! Hee hee! I guess we're two kindred spirits with two fiery passions!

Quentin let out another deep, emotional sigh. "Amazing... I've never seen a proof of pact so perfect—one single loop with no breaks!"

He rolled his left sleeve up to his elbow and thrust his arm out in front of me. "Please, behold my proof of pact! It took eighty knights to subjugate that monster—an A-Rank monster, I might add—and make it my familiar."

A line coiled around his arm several times like a snake, stretching from his wrist to his elbow. It started about three centimeters wide at his wrist, then grew to more than twice that. It looked like the line continued even past his elbow, though his uniform covered the rest. The line itself seemed scaly—a far cry from the solid, unbroken one around my wrist.

He laughed. "I've always thought that a long proof of pact like mine was normal for an A-rank monster, but after seeing yours, I feel ridiculous. Yours is so narrow..." Quentin sounded entranced. "A single, unbroken loop. One millimeter thick. Absolute obedience..."

He deflated, slumping his huge body onto the table. For a while he just stayed like that—and then, suddenly, he jolted up and grabbed my left hand. "Please, tell me how in sync you are with your familiar! Your proof of pact is perfect! Is that useful to you? I need to know! I know you can't tell me everything, but please! Anything! Even a little bit! How'd you do it?!"

Well, he did look pretty sincere. *Yeah. I get ya, Captain Quentin. Any good expert wants to keep learning.*

"Um, sure! I happened to come across my familiar when he was really, really hurt, so I fed him a healing potion I had on hand. Then he offered to become my familiar. It was something about how his kind devotes their lives to their saviors, I think?"

"Inconceivable. Even if it reverted to infancy, I can't imagine the Black Dr—dra...*drinking*...the potion...would make sense? Because I can't imagine *your* familiar ever getting injured in the first place! And you healed it like that?! Where its own superior natural recovery failed, *you* managed to heal the beast? Such a thing shouldn't be possible..." Quentin put his elbows on the table and ruffled his hair. "What happened then?! How in sync are you two?!"

"Let's see...I think he can hear me no matter how far apart we are and come right to me. He always listens to what I say, and sometimes he even acts on stuff I haven't said out loud. He never does anything I wouldn't want, though, and...we've only been together for a short while, but he seems to know what I was doing while we were apart."

Quentin snapped his fingers as if something had clicked into place for him. "Of course! That hole in the sky opened because you called him! But just how synchronized are you two? I...I... As powerful as you are, Miss Fia, you probably consider it beneath you to know all about your mighty familiar. Would it be acceptable if I questioned your familiar directly? Of course, you needn't tell me anything more than you wish!"

"Huh? Um, I'll ask."

I called out to Zavilia—he was roosting in my uniform as usual. He popped his head out from beneath my collar and stared at Quentin. After a while, he left my uniform and perched on my knees.

"I heard from Patty that your voice box is damaged," said Quentin earnestly. "Your cries sound like a human's voice. Please, feel free to speak to me!"

My hand came to a stop in the middle of petting Zavilia. *This is pretty weird, isn't it?* It was like Quentin had seen through Zavilia's disguise and knew how powerful he actually was. I didn't *think* he knew about Zavilia being a black dragon. Then again, he'd mentioned that hole in the sky, and he'd talked about Zavilia reverting to infancy.

Yeah...it wasn't impossible that the captain of the Fourth Monster Tamer Knight Brigade figured out what Zavilia was. I could keep playing dumb, or I could come clean and try to get more information about Zavilia. Hmm...

I met Quentin's eyes. He looked back at me silently, full poker face. My brain chugged and chugged until suddenly a flash of brilliance came to me.

Quentin's silence itself is a sign, isn't it? He's figured out that Zavilia's a black dragon, but he hasn't directly stated it—he's suggesting that we keep it secret! Oh, but of course! If he admits he knows, he'll be forced to report it! That'll just cause trouble for both Zavilia and me. I read you loud and clear, Cap'n!

I smiled at him. "He'll answer if he feels like answering. Feel free to ask away, Captain Quentin."

Zavilia made a sour face, but he looked to Quentin regardless. **"You wished to ask me something?"**

"Y-yes! Firstly, allow me to say it is an honor to be graced with your voice. It's akin to the thunder of an angel's trumpet, to the gentle burble of a mermaid swimming in a desert oasis, to—"

"That's enough," Zavilia snapped. **"I don't know what you're on about, but I don't care to chat with anyone besides Fia. Can we cut the pleasantries?"**

Quentin straightened in his chair. "Y-yes! Forgive me! May I ask for more details about your relationship with Miss Fia?"

"You may. We're close. We have what you called 'absolute obedience.' It links our health and magic together, though it's only a one-way flow from me to Fia. If her health or magic fail, my own strength replenishes hers. So long as I live, she cannot die. So long as my magic lasts, she cannot suffer magic fatigue."

"Pfft?!" Surprised, I spat out the water I was drinking...and I spat it far. The water even reached Quentin and doused his face. "C-Captain Quentin?! I just sprayed you with water. Um. Shouldn't you say something?! I, uh—I'll go fetch a towel!"

But Quentin barely seemed to notice as he waited for Zavilia's next words. "Thank you, Miss Fia, but you need not concern yourself with me." He turned back to Zavilia. "More importantly, thank you for sharing this fascinating information! I had no idea transferring health and magic was even *possible*. I take it that Fia cannot transfer health and magic to you?"

"Not unless she wills it. Her actions, thoughts, and emotions also flow into me no matter how far apart we may be. Thus, I always know what my master is doing and how she regards her surroundings, allowing me to take my own actions as her familiar."

"Pffft?!" Here I was thinking I could drink some cool, refreshing water to calm myself down, and he drops *that* on me? Poor Quentin got another blast as he leaned forward, a fascinated look in his eyes. "T-twice?! C-Captain Quentin, forgive me! I-I'll go fetch a towel for real this time!"

"No need, Miss Fia. No need at all. Not when we're having such an important conversation," he said, stony-faced. "Still, this is quite a lot to process. You know what your master is doing even when you're apart?" (Drip, drip.) "You can even read her thoughts and feelings?"

"And a good thing too. Otherwise I'd have to ask her all sorts of questions directly. For instance: 'How badly do you want to beat that Gideon jerk running his mouth? Within an inch of his life? Or would you prefer a millimeter?' Things like that."

Quentin froze. He began laughing in an unnatural, shrill voice. "G-G-Gideon, you say? Ha ha ha, what a coincidence! My, uh, vice-captain has the same name."

"Are there any other Gideons we know besides your idiotic vice-captain? Don't play dumb."

"Y-yes, yes, my apologies! I'm so very sorry for the trouble he's caused you!" he said, bowing his head deeply.

No, no, no, you're not at fault at all! Please raise your head! If a well-known captain like you bows to me, we'll draw everyone's attention! Oh no, everyone's looking at us now!

Flustered, I tried to get Quentin to raise his head when a man approached from behind him, putting a hand on his shoulder. "There you are, Quentin. C'mon now. Let's go."

Quentin blinked a few times as though waking from a dream, and then he looked up at the man. "H-huh? Oh, right. The captains' meeting." He hurriedly stood. Paused. "U-um, I'd hate to impose on you, Miss Fia," he said hesitantly, "but would you be willing to attend the meeting with me?"

"Huh? Um, sure! If that's okay." I stood up, and the other man finally noticed me.

"Oh! Well, if it ain't Fia. What're you doing here?"

"Good afternoon, Captain Desmond. It's been a while." I greeted Desmond, captain of the Second Knight Brigade, with a smile.

A Tale of the
Secret
Saint

The Captains' Meeting

DESMOND OPENED HIS MOUTH to say something, but instead, he just shook his head. "There's a lot I'm dying to ask right now. 'Why is Quentin soaking wet,' for instance? Or maybe 'Why is Quentin prioritizing lunch with Fia over the captains' meeting?' But there's no time. I'll question you two later. For now, hurry up and get moving!" Desmond gestured back to the entrance of the canteen before storming off, clearly expecting us to follow.

"*Ugh*. It's odd to see Quentin running late. Is Fia doing something again?" I heard Desmond click his tongue, and I could almost swear that he muttered my name, but I couldn't quite make out anything else.

Quentin and I hurried after Desmond. Zavilia returned to his usual roost underneath my uniform and nuzzled against my belly. *Back to sleep, buddy?* I gave Zavilia a gentle pat through my top.

Eventually, we reached the Knight Brigade's main building. We walked down the long hallway, passing many knights going about their knightly business, before reaching a remarkably ornate double door. Two knights opened it as we approached, revealing a wide room. Tall glass windows lined the wall facing the courtyard, bathing the room in light. A large, grandiose round table stood in the center of the room. A number of knights sat in chairs around it.

"Cutting it close, aren't ya, Quentin?" From among the sitting knights, an auburn-haired man stood up and spoke. He approached a few steps before noticing me standing behind Quentin. "Oh, Fia! It's been a while! How've you been?"

"Huh?" I blurted, not recognizing the man. I saw the sash hanging diagonally across his chest and finally remembered.

Oh, right. That night of the Flower-Horned Deer meat party, there was that guy glaring at the Unit Three guys—it's him!

"Good afternoon, Captain Zackary," I said. "I have been well." The way he called out to me like we were friends really surprised me—he probably mistook me for someone else—but I managed an inoffensive reply. We'd never talked before, so I didn't want to make things awkward.

"Ha ha ha! Are you not gonna call me 'Zackary,' like before?" he said, tousling my hair.

Ow, hey! You're messing my hair up! I don't know who you're mistaking me for, but I'm not gonna address a captain without their title!

Zackary just bent down and put his arm around my neck, pulling me closer. "C'mon, don't be a stranger! We shared all that risqué scuttlebutt about the Commander, eh?" he whispered in my ear. "Drop the formalities already!"

Wait, what?! That sounds so...so indecent! *Just what kind of nut job is he mistaking me for?!*

I tried to stammer out a reply, but Zackary had already turned his attention to Quentin. "And your hair, Quentin? All wet and drippy...what, did you go for a dip in a lake?"

"This? Miss Fia sprayed water on me with her mouth," said Quentin matter-of-factly.

Zackary snapped his head back at me and hysterically blared, "Fia, you're into *that* kind of stuff?!"

"I am *not*!" I snapped. *Y-you can't just say things like that, Captain Quentin! And c'mon, Captain Zackary! Stop yelling! Everyone's looking over here now!*

I tried to explain it was a misunderstanding, but Zackary's booming voice drowned me out. "Accident?! Bah! You'd have to *try* to soak someone this bad!"

Without even waiting for my reply, Zackary turned to Quentin. "And what's with you, Quentin?! At least try to dry yourself off—or do you like being this wet?!"

Who in the world would enjoy being wet?! I wondered, flabbergasted.

I heard the knights around us begin to whisper, saying all kinds of things—"Did you hear Quentin just now? He called that girl 'Miss'! He's definitely a masochist." *Wha—hold up! People can say whatever they want about Captain Quentin, but at this rate, people are gonna start throwing me in with him too! Oria would blow a gasket if that happened! And...what's that icy glare I'm feeling from my right? That's gotta be Captain Cyril. Can't check, can't look, no way! Eek! If I don't clear this up now, he's gonna give me the scolding of a lifetime!*

"Captain Quentin! Ha! Uh, why don't we clear up this misunderstanding? I just *happened* to choke during our lunch and spat my water out, right?"

"Huh?!" Zackary sounded shocked. "Quentin, you ate lunch together?! I thought you made it a rule to not eat with women, even from your own brigade?!"

Huh? No, no, no! That rule is way too specific! Now nobody's going to believe me!

My mind worked overtime on ways out of my predicament when Quentin started explaining, wearing a strange and spellbound expression. "Miss Fia was the one who invited me, so there was no way I could refuse. It also isn't quite correct to say that we ate lunch together. Although we sat together, I wouldn't dare to eat in her presence. Still, our lunch together was wonderful. Priceless, even. She even allowed me to touch her left arm as much as I pleased. Even when she spat on me, I was grateful. It brought me to my senses during a wondrous moment."

The other knights recoiled at Quentin's strange expression and deeply concerning words. Even I was creeped out—who wouldn't be after hearing he enjoyed touching my left arm and getting doused with spit-water?

I took a step forward. "Just stop! Phrasing, man! You're making it sound like you're some kind of weird...*wet arm pervert*!"

"I-I'm sorry, Miss Fia!" he blustered. "Please don't be angry with me, I beg you!"

"That's it! Stop that! Just don't say *anything*! Think about how I feel about all this!" I yelled at the top of my lungs.

Just then, a low baritone voice spoke from behind me. "Enjoying yourself, Fia? Whenever things get noisy in my vicinity, I always seem to find you."

Saviz had entered the room. It seemed he'd come after being told that everyone was in attendance.

"C-Commander Saviz! Help me!" I squeaked. C'mon, be my knight in shining armor?

He raised an eyebrow. "What is it?"

I ran up to him, elated that he'd listen. Sure, it was strange for a recruit to ask their commander for help, but who else could I turn to? Before anyone could reprimand me for my conduct, I explained the situation.

"So, *ahem*...so! I just *happened* to come across Captain Quentin and eat lunch with him because we were both on our way to the canteen, but during said lunch, I accidentally spat water on him because I heard something crazy, which *was* my fault, okay? Okay! But now Captain Quentin is recounting what happened all weirdly, and it makes us look like a pair of water-spitting arm perverts, and now everybody's got the wrong idea! Please, do something! I think Captain Quentin's bad at explaining stuff, maybe?!"

Saviz listened without interruption and, when I was done, gave an understanding nod. "My most talented knights always do the strangest things in your presence. Perhaps it's a sort of natural reaction to your own absurdity. Quentin is surely tired after such a long expedition. He'll doubtless soon be back to normal."

"Thank you very much, Commander Saviz!" I said. Smugly, I looked around. *You hear that everyone?! Quentin's just tired from his expedition!*

Just when I was feeling drained by all the chaos, I heard a refreshingly calm voice call out to me. "Looks like everything worked out for you. Why don't you come over here?" Cyril smiled gently at me, beckoning me over. "We're allowed to bring up to two subordinates to the captains' meeting. I came alone this time. Why don't you join me? You're in my brigade, after all."

I looked around and, sure enough, there was a knight or two standing behind each captain at the round table. I was about to walk over to Cyril when someone grabbed my arm—Quentin.

"What are you saying, Cyril? I'm the one who brought Fia. Besides, she's helping my brigade at the moment. She should obviously stay with me."

Cyril narrowed his eyes at Quentin. He did not stop smiling.

I-Incredible, Captain Cyril! So perfectly unnerving! He's style, he's grace, that's a flawless scary face!

Zackary cackled. "Looks like you'll offend someone no matter who you go with, Fia! Why not come stay by me?"

H-huh? I just deescalated the last situation, so why am I getting wrapped up in a whole new one?!

Stunned at the development before me, I stood still as a statue.

Saviz looked amused. "Well then, Fia...what would you like to do?"

Um...can I go home?

I pulled myself together and scanned the table, considering my options.

It seemed like today's meeting was just for the brigades within the royal capital—you could tell because four seats were filled, even though there were enough chairs for all twenty brigade captains plus the commander. Saviz, Quentin, and Zackary were in attendance, of course, but they were currently standing near me. Of the four sitting, I recognized two—my brigade captain Cyril and Second Knight Brigade Captain Desmond. I hadn't seen the other two knights before, but I could make some guesses from the color of their sashes. The long-haired man was probably Enoch, captain of the Third Mage Knight Brigade, and the woman might've been Clarissa, captain of the Fifth Knight Brigade that led the royal capital's defense.

My eyes went wide the moment I saw Clarissa. Amidst all the tall, hulking men, she stood out. Her wavy, peach-pink hair coiled around her face. It highlighted her spotless skin, her large, amber eyes that sparkled like gems, and her full lips—they were the same peach-pink as her hair. I was surprised to discover we had such a beautiful captain, but not as surprised as I was to see that humongous chest of hers. It totally defied her stuffy uniform! The top buttons of her uniform were daringly left undone, revealing a shirt underneath that was also unbuttoned, further revealing some deep cleavage. I mean, not even *Desmond* kept those unbuttoned.

Then it hit me. *Wait, no! She isn't leaving her uniform unbuttoned, she* can't *button her uniform! Blessed with looks and a killer body...this is the ultimate form I must aim for!*

"Beautiful..." I murmured as I staggered closer to her. *Whoa, she smells so sweet!*

I heard Zackary's frantic voice from behind me. "F-Fia, no! Don't be deceived! That *thing* you're approaching is the knight brigades' cruelest and most merciless knight! She's only pretending to be weak! And she's totally older than she looks!"

Cyril stood and spoke gravely. "Zackary is correct! Fia, they call that woman the Pink Praying Mantis! Countless young knights have fallen for her, despite knowing her deadly reputation. Men, women...everyone! Heed our warning!"

Hey now, that's no way to talk about your fellow captain! Besides, I'm sick and tired of being surrounded by buff, sweaty men! I much prefer a sweet-smelling lady, you know?

"I choose to stay with the Fifth Knight Brigade Captain!" I declared.

"You don't even know her!" everyone shouted at once, but I paid them no mind.

I performed the knight salute and greeted Clarissa. "I am Fia Ruud of the First Knight Brigade. Please allow me to stand behind you for the duration of the captains' meeting."

She batted her wide, long-lashed eyes a few times before breaking into a dazzling smile that I could only compare to a blooming flower. "My, how wonderful! I'm Clarissa Abernethy, captain of the Fifth Knight Brigade. A pleasure."

Eeeee, even her voice is cute? The way the ends of her sentences inflect upward is wonderful too? I'm hooked?!

Seeing that I had made my choice, Saviz moved to begin the meeting. Everyone stood up, waited for Saviz to be seated, and then sat back down themselves.

"We will now begin the captains' meeting," the meeting moderator announced.

The captains' meeting was held on a pretty regular basis, but this one was called suddenly due to Quentin's return. The meeting started off by going over their brigades' plans for the month and a quick discussion of the budget, then they moved on to the main item on the agenda.

Cyril, presiding over the meeting, introduced the next topic. "Let us move on to the matter of the Black Dragon King. Originally, the plan was to determine the new location of the Black King and mobilize a team of three hundred knights. This team, formed primarily from the Fourth and Sixth Knight Brigades, was to capture it while it was still in its infant form. However, a sighting in Starfall Forest leads us to believe the Black Dragon King has grown faster than we anticipated. Quentin, do you have anything to add on the matter?"

"Yes. We must change our plans. Capturing the Black Dragon King is no longer possible now that it has grown. Our best course of action is to restore the ecosystem's balance by ensuring the Black Dragon King's return to its nest on Blackpeak Mountain."

"Damn, and just when I thought we'd get our first big catch in a while," Zackary groaned. "How many people will you need?"

Quentin pondered that for a moment, running his long fingers through his hair. "We can't bring too many. If the Black Dragon King thinks we're a threat, things won't end well. Perhaps...fifteen from my brigade and thirty-five from the Sixth Knight Brigade?"

Clarissa cut in. "Oh my, how scary! *Do* be careful. We wouldn't want the Black Dragon King to accidently meander its way into the capital. Why, I might get a little grumpy if my cute wittle citizens are in danger."

"We'll be careful, then," Zackary said curtly and continued. "The Black Dragon King may have wandered into Starfall Forest. Its memories might not have fully settled, you see, after its rebirth. Quentin, you brought back some rocks and a piece of its corpse from its nest, right? You think it'll regain its memories and return to its nest if you show them those?"

Quentin looked downcast. "It's...worth a shot." He briefly glanced up at me, and we exchanged a look.

I read you loud and clear, Captain Quentin! We'll have Zavilia appear while you're searching Starfall Forest, then he'll fly off toward his nest after you throw a rock at him!

I peeked down my collar at Zavilia to see him still snoring it up on my belly.

Heh heh! Kids sure do sleep a lot. Yeah, I'm sure Zavilia will be fine with the plan.

I smiled back at Quentin, signaling that I got the message, when Cyril suddenly cut in with some spiky words. "Quentin, could you not give my subordinate these licentious sidelong glances? Such behavior is most improper in a meeting."

"We're merely signaling each other, Cyril," said Quentin. "I asked her if she would accompany me on the search for the Black Dragon King and she agreed. Oh—I've only known Miss Fia for a day, and we can still understand each other through glances alone! And oh, it looks like *you* can't. Remind me," he said with a mocking grin, "how long have you known her now?"

Cyril narrowed his eyes and flashed that same razor-edge smile.

Whoa—hey! Cut it out, you two! Stop bickering like kids! I thought, bewildered by their sudden hostility toward one another.

Clarissa watched the two men quarrel and giggled. "Somebody's a popular girl. But you're still a little green around the edges. You need to tease them more, dear. Leave them at the brink, wanting more and more until they're left *begging* when you stop."

Desmond groaned. "What'd I tell you?! It's always women who cause trouble!"

As for Enoch, he remained silent.

Zackary's eyes flicked around the table, and then he slammed his hands down. "Give it a rest! You're in the presence of Commander Saviz!" Zackary glared at the now-silent captains. "It's settled, then. We embark tomorrow morning. I'll bring thirty-five from my brigade, and Quentin will bring fifteen. Of course, we'll both be participating ourselves. Any objections?"

After waiting a moment, the captains all turned toward Saviz. He nodded once. "Very well," he said. "Don't push yourselves."

It was decided—we would depart the next morning.

Without warning, the captains all rose in unison and put a fist over their hearts. I followed suit, along with the other knights in attendance behind their captains.

Saviz rose last and spoke in a clear, sonorous voice. "Glory to the Náv Black Dragon Knights."

"Glory to the Náv Black Dragon Knights!" we chanted back.

Saviz left the room, and the captains' meeting came to an end.

A Tale of the
Secret
Saint

The Search for the Black Dragon Part 1

I WOKE UP EARLIER than usual the next morning, probably because I was excited about the Starfall Forest expedition. Recruits like me weren't eligible to be part of the main force—and I wasn't when I tagged along with the Sixth Knight Brigade on the monster extermination either—but they still let me join by Quentin's request.

Training and looking after familiars was important and all, but getting into the field? That's where it's at!

The expedition was organized on short notice, so there was no time to send an official request to the church to ask for saints. Instead, we'd be accompanied by some who were stationed within the Royal Castle.

The fifteen knights from the Fourth Monster Tamer Knight Brigade would bring their familiars, and I was looking forward to finally seeing how people with familiars fought. I'd only seen monsters as something to be defeated in my past life, so it still seemed novel that people were teaming up with them.

I finished my preparations and picked up Zavilia. He was the star of the show today, so I made sure he was dressed to impress!

"Um...Fia? I'm fine with wearing a ribbon on my neck, but the flowers on my head are...well, are they truly necessary?"

"Of course they are! You're the cutest familiar ever, and we'll leverage that cuteness to get the respect from all fifteen of the other familiars!"

"I could smack them around, you know. That would earn me respect."

"No, no, no! Then you'd just be another run-of-the-mill *strong* familiar. They gotta understand how cute you are!"

"I...see. How very complicated."

I lifted Zavilia up to my shoulder and let him perch there before finally leaving the room. A yellow flower crown was fitted on his head, and a bright red ribbon around his neck added a splash of color.

I arrived at the meeting area extra-early, but I was far from the first one there. I recognized some familiar faces from the Sixth Knight Brigade and called out to them. "Good morning!"

"Hey, it's Fia! Morning! Ha ha, nice to know you're coming along with us!"

I talked with them for a while, and before I knew it, most of the remaining knights had arrived. Everyone was pretty beefy, overshadowing me in both width and height, but Zackary and Quentin were the buffest of the buff. They gave off this overwhelming sense of presence.

Hmm...they say that if you want to hide a tree, put it in a forest, but I don't think you could put these two great oaks anywhere with-out 'em standing out. If anything, standing next to normal knights only makes these guys more *conspicuous. It's a good thing I'm just a sapling.* Yeah, it was good that I didn't stand out.

At that moment, Quentin began pacing straight toward me, and the surrounding knights started to murmur.

"Good morning, Miss Fia," he said, "and good morning to your esteemed familiar as well. Thank you for coming so early in the morning."

"Good morning, Captain Quentin. How'd you notice me so fast over all these tall knights?" I asked.

He gave a hearty laugh as though my question were a joke. "Very funny, Miss Fia! As if I could fail to notice a presence as strong as yours. We will be having a meeting shortly. Would you care to join?"

I nodded, prompting Quentin to walk back to where Zackary was. As soon as he left, the surrounding knights began pelting me with questions.

"Fia, do you two know each other or somethin'?! I thought he had nothing but monsters on his mind! This is the first time I've seen him talk to anyone from another brigade!" a knight said.

"Forget that, I wanna know why he's calling you '*Miss* Fia'!" another knight said.

"I'd say she's less a *Miss* to Quentin and way more of a *Mistress*," Zackary cut in, to my dismay.

Ugh, what was with Captain Quentin and Captain Zackary always causing misunderstandings?!

"O-oh, I see...a *Mistress*, huh?" a knight mumbled thoughtfully.

"But Captain Quentin is big, strong, and intimidating," a knight said to me. "That's like, your polar opposite. Is he really your type?"

Were the knights really going to so readily accept Zackary's explanation? C'mon! Sure, he was their captain, but most people wouldn't take such a statement at face value...right?

I followed Zackary to where Quentin was. Gideon was there too, standing beside him.

"Miss Fia!" Quentin greeted me. "Thank you for entertaining my invitation."

Uh...*hmm*. The way Quentin talked struck me as pretty weird. Sure, I wasn't always the biggest stickler for hierarchy, but he absolutely outranked me. The polite way he talked to me seemed, quite frankly, wrong...but what could I do? A mere recruit like me had no right to speak out about his tone. It would be different if he were like Cyril, who spoke politely to everyone—but wait, speaking of Cyril, didn't he and Quentin say something about *playing* when I first met Quentin? Was that what Quentin was doing? Playing some kind of game?

What was this guy's deal?

I let out a small sigh, but Zackary's booming voice drowned it out. "I see your odd way of addressing Fia still hasn't changed, Quentin. I expect that from Cyril, but seeing you talk to anyone other than the Commander like that just creeps me out! Rather inauspicious way to start a mission, don't you think?"

"*Hmph!* You're just too dull, Zackary!" Quentin snapped. "Why, every one of you should see Miss Fia's magnificence!"

Zackary looked doubtful. "Sure, I'm a bit dull, but Fia? *Magnificent?*" Zackary beckoned Gideon over to whisper in his ear. "Hey, is your captain for real? Should we give him a good shake to wake him up or somethin'?"

Gideon shook his head. "I doubt that'd work, sir. I've never seen the Captain like this before. Even *I* don't know what to do."

Wow. So Gideon can show proper respect when talking to superiors.

"We'll...ignore the issue for now!" Zackary declared, sounding a bit defeated. "Sit down, it's time for a strategy meeting!"

He pointed to a simple table and some chairs in the corner of the meeting area before sitting down himself. We took our seats, and Zackary kicked off the four-person meeting.

"We've prepared supplies for a week's worth of camping. I've picked my thirty-five best knights for the mission. If things get hairy with the Black King, you can be assured that we'll carry our weight."

"Good," said Quentin. "I selected my knights based on the familiars we'd need for the mission. Ten are capable of flight, and the remaining five familiars are flightless. The ten I chose should prove useful in guiding the Black Dragon King to its nest, when the time comes."

Zackary nodded. "Not bad. Any idea what our chances are when it comes to actually finding the Black Dragon King? Ten percent? Less, I suspect. Trying to find a single monster in that forest is like trying to find a needle in a haystack. It's quite possible the beast has already flown the coop."

"It is one hundred percent certain," Quentin said.

Zackary blinked. *"What?"*

"There's a hundred percent chance we'll find the Black Dragon King," Quentin repeated with utter confidence.

"I'm not asking how much you *want* to meet the Black King! Temper your expectations a bit, would you?" Zackary gave Quentin a slap on the shoulder before continuing. "Now, then—the plan is to approach the Black Dragon King from outside of its attack range. Hmm, yes...we should avoid encircling it. We don't want to appear threatening, after all. Once we're in place, you'll convince it to return to its nest—it should be able to understand human words with its intellect, right? Once you've convinced it, we'll take a stone from its nest or a piece of its old corpse. We'll have a familiar hold onto it and send it off in the direction of Blackpeak Mountain. But I doubt things will go exactly as planned, so we'll have to adjust on the fly."

"Sounds good," Quentin replied. "We should also avoid other monsters as much as possible. The local ecosystem is already in chaos with the appearance of the Black Dragon King—we might even come across rarer deep-forest monsters. Things should settle down once the Black King leaves. Until then, we should avoid any direct confrontation."

"Understood. I'll pass that on to the scout lead," Zackary said as he stood up and rustled my hair. "But there's no way we can *completely* avoid monsters. We'll have to fight where we must and adapt where we can. As for you, Fia...I've heard you played a role in the last expedition, but this time, I want you to stay on the sidelines. There's a chance we might come across a high-rank monster, after all."

Can't argue against that...or at least, not with sword skills like mine. Sir, yes, sir! Fia will be a good little knight and watch from the sidelines! I nodded obediently, somehow earning a weary sigh from Zavilia.

What? Doesn't he believe me?

"Eh heh heh! Zavilia, you're *suuuch* a cutie!"

The saints were to arrive later, same as last time, which left me plenty of free time to greet the other familiars. It was time for Zavilia's long-awaited debut into familiar society!

I adjusted the ribbon around his neck—had to make sure he made a good first impression with the other familiars, after all. Just looking at the little ribbon reminded me of how darling he was!

"You've always been adorable, but the ribbon and flowers? Downright *precious*!"

"Thank you. Over the long years of my ancient existence, you are the first to call me things like 'adorable' and 'precious.'"

"Heh heh! Ancient? You're only zero years old!" I said, perching Zavilia on my shoulder and beginning to walk toward the other familiars. "Whoa..."

I couldn't hide my surprise once I laid eyes on them. Each and every familiar stood so tall and gallant. Quentin must've really chosen the best of the best for the job. A particularly large and graceful-looking familiar caught my eye: a creature with golden wings, the head of a hawk, and the body of a lion—a griffon.

Oh...that must be Quentin's familiar. A glance was all I needed to see that the griffon was a good step above the other familiars strength-wise—it was probably A-rank. I couldn't peel my eyes away. Its beauty was captivating...but I came here with a purpose.

"Nice to meet you, I am Fia Ruud of the First Knight Brigade. And this is my familiar, Zav..." I hesitated, remembering Quentin's warning.

Uhh, shoot. Captain Quentin told me not to tell anybody Zavilia's name, but did familiars count? I...better place it safe. "And, uh, this is my own little 'Blue Dragon of Happiness!'" Yeah, that'd work. Just like "The Bluebird of Happiness."

I spoke as politely as I could, seeing as a griffon should be capable of understanding human speech. Then I approached it with my hands open, showing I meant well. It looked cautious as I approached, but it didn't seem aggressive.

Quentin was kind of like this when we first met too. Like master, like familiar, eh? As I came closer, though, I noticed how strangely it was standing. *Hm? It's injured...*

It avoided putting weight on its back foot, and its wing was fractured. It must not have had enough time to heal—Quentin *had* just gotten back from that expedition, after all.

I could really respect the familiar for that. I mean, here it was, embarking on a new mission despite not being fully ready. Unless...Quentin was forcing it? He wouldn't, would he?

Too bad you weren't around to drink the green healing potion yesterday, I thought as I placed a hand on its leg.

"Heal!" I cast my magic, doing my best to suppress the light it gave off.

Okay...with this, it should look like I'm just petting the griffon. Nothing to see here!

"People can't usually just walk up casually to a griffon and give it a pet, Fia," Zavilia warned me gently. **"They might be weak compared to what you fought in your past life, but they're high-ranking monsters. I'm surprised it let you touch it at all..."**

Sorry, Zavilia. I saw the injury and started healing before I knew it. At least it was just a monster instead of a person. Shouldn't blow my cover—right, Zavilia?

The griffon nuzzled its large head against me, taking me by surprise...and the other familiars around me started letting out low growls. I scanned the group, and sure enough, many of them were injured too. I didn't recognize any of them from the familiar stables, so maybe they'd been on that expedition with Quentin? If so, they were probably totally wiped.

I went around, placing a hand on them and healing them just like I'd healed the griffon. Their injuries varied a lot in severity, but it was no trouble healing them all.

Before I knew it, I found myself surrounded by the familiars. Before I could even yelp with surprise, they closed in and nuzzled against my body.

Wh-what's going on?!

The word "cute" didn't feel like the right word for such large familiars, but...ehh, close enough!

"You healed them. Of course they've warmed up to you..."

Zavilia turned away with a huff. **"Must be nice having monsters fawn over you again."**

Aww, is he sulking? I gave Zavilia some head pats. "You'll always be the cutest in my heart! You're the only one who could ever rock a ribbon and a flower crown like that!"

"Hmph." He didn't sound wholly dissatisfied, at least?

Whoops. I forgot how jealous kids can get.

I was petting the familiars around me, trying to bring them under control, when I heard a voice from behind me. "M-Miss Fia?"

I turned around to see Quentin and Gideon standing there with looks of shock on their faces, because...why? It took a moment to hit me—

"Ah! Is there a rule against touching other people's familiars?! I'm sorry!" I immediately tried to distance myself from the familiars, who purred sadly. I felt bad, but I didn't want to risk another scolding. If they were that upset, I must've really crossed the line.

I approached Quentin and Gideon slowly, stopping *juuuust* far enough away to bolt if needed—but it wasn't far enough, because Quentin closed the distance in a few steps and grabbed my hands.

"Eeeek!" I shrieked. "I'm sorry!"

"Fia!" Quentin exclaimed. "Are you a taming prodigy?!"

"A ta—a—*huh*?" I looked up at him in confusion, only to be met with a fierce glare. *"Eep!* You're angry after all!"

I tried to pull my hands away and flee, but no dice. It didn't *seem* like he was holding me that tightly, but I couldn't budge no matter how hard I pulled. *Hnnnng!*

"I've always thought familiars never warmed up to anyone but their masters, but all of them are nuzzling against you like a horde of puppies!" Quentin groaned. "My knowledge is clearly so superficial. I'm not fit to be Fourth Monster Tamer Knight Brigade's captain!"

"Huh?" I blinked. "Um, aren't you exaggerating a bit much?"

It wasn't weird for Quentin to be weird, but now he seemed genuinely ashamed to be a captain at all. His face was scrunched up something nasty. I tried to reassure him and looked around for help, meeting Gideon's gaze.

His eyes went wide with surprise as they met mine. He approached rapidly, much like Quentin had a moment ago, but didn't seem as hostile as usual. What, was he coming to help cheer Quentin up or something? But no—instead he stopped before me and bowed his head deeply.

"Please excuse my actions up until now!"

"*Whuh?*" One surprise after another...

"Captain Quentin informed me that your visit to our brigade was a direct order from the Commander! He likely had his reasons, even if I didn't understand them at the time. Only now do I truly understand! How could I be so *foolish*?!"

"Huh? Um..."

"I took my own grudge against the other brigades out on you! Please, allow me to step down from my position as vice-captain as an apology!"

"Okay, *stoooop*!" I yelled. What was Gideon on about? Out of all the weird things he'd blurted out all of a sudden, the weirdest had to be the last bit. Sure, he'd made some snide remarks, but they didn't bother me that much.

What reason are you even going to give for that kinda resignation? Hi, yes, I was so mean to a recruit that I gotta step down? Really?!

I was about to speak out, hopefully to change Gideon's mind, when I heard a voice from behind me.

"What in the *world* are you guys doing?" There Zackary stood, arms crossed and looking utterly confused. "Quentin holding Fia's hands, Gideon taking a knee like he's begging for something... what, are you two fighting over Fia?!"

Zackary's words brought me down to earth. Yeah, it *was* kind of weird: Quentin still grasped my hands with no signs of letting go, and Gideon had somehow bowed his head to the point where he was outright kneeling.

"H-how long have you been there?!"

But Zackary ignored my question, instead just shaking his head in exasperation. "A new follower already, *Queen* Fia? You're really something..."

"N-n-no! It's not like that, Captain Zackary!"

"Don't worry, I understand. You'll break somebody's heart no matter who you choose. Here," he said, pulling me away from the two. "Let me help. Their Graces have arrived, and you two better make sure not to offend them. Just imagine them as a couple of Fias, why don't you? Show them all the respect they deserve, got it?!"

His choice of example struck me as weird, but at least I could finally get back to the others.

Too bad we didn't get to finish introducing you to the other familiars, Zavilia. Seven saints had arrived, but Charlotte wasn't one of them. *Figures. They wouldn't send a girl as young as her, would they?*

We split into three units to move faster—two of fifteen and one of twenty—and we'd periodically blow our whistles to gauge our distance from the others. Quentin and Gideon each lead one of the units and insisted I join theirs, but Zackary swooped in and let me join his instead. *Thank goodness.*

And so we made our way into Starfall Forest, knights, familiars, and a few horses and carriages alongside.

Wow, I've been coming to this forest a lot lately. Then, suddenly, it hit me. *Wait...this expedition's about finding a black dragon, right? So it won't end until then. But* when *should I have Zavilia appear? Now...would be too soon, right? Shoot! I should've settled on a time with Quentin!*

I wondered for a while...maybe I could ask him at lunch? Zackary brought enough supplies for a week, so I didn't need to rush things.

We came across our first monster ten minutes after entering the forest—a beautiful bird that shone with rainbow colors.

"You're kidding me!" Zackary exclaimed. "What's a Dream Bird doing so close to the entrance?" I couldn't blame him for being shocked. Sure, its vivid colors were pretty to look at, but it was a difficult monster to fight. The thing could even produce illusions. Usually, you'd find them way deeper in the forest. Its actual combat power was low, but its illusions messed with your spatial awareness something awful. If things went wrong, it wasn't just hard to attack; you could wind up whacking your allies with your own weapons!

By Zackary's orders, four archers and three mages started blasting away at the monster, but they couldn't land a decent hit.

Zackary told me to "stay on the sidelines" earlier and appointed me to guard the saints, and so I did just that. Just...stood by the saints, spectating.

Funny. I thought all mages were assigned to the Third Mage Knight Brigade, but I guess not? Weird that I didn't notice sooner. The mages didn't use anything but detection magic last expedition, so I guess that's why I hadn't noticed who they were. How interesting, to consider how roles could change so quickly when a new leader took charge. Truly fascinating, how those changed roles affected what strategy was most viable for any given situation!

Just riveting!

Oh my God, I'm so bored, I can barely focus.

I frowned and looked at Zackary, who was currently in combat. *The Dream Bird's a B-rank, if I remember right.* I watched the monster flutter above me, keeping its distance from the knights, and thought up my own strategy.

As a general rule, you gotta kill Dream Birds as quickly as you can. If you give them enough time to fly in a complete circle, anyone caught inside falls victim to its illusions. Once that happens, its color changes from rainbow to solid green, and it transforms into the A-rank monster Green Nightmare. Its attack and defense fly way up, but it doesn't lose its illusions powers either. Most knights can't even scratch it after that, so now was their only chance.

I watched as the monster traced a circle, dipped in the air, and rocketed back up.

Ah. Too late.

I bit my lip as I watched the knights fall victim to illusion. Sight, hearing, even smell...all of their senses were ensnared. They lost sense of their surroundings, their eyes darting about wildly before finally landing on the Dream Bird that was now swelling in size.

That, unfortunately, was no illusion. Feather by feather, its color began to change, its plumage morphing into scaly green skin. In no time at all, it had become more giant lizard than beautiful bird—a Green Nightmare.

The Green Nightmare let out a piercing wail before kicking off the earth with its long, thick legs, barreling toward the knights. The fact that its body couldn't fly anymore was a pretty crappy consolation prize for the *new* fact that it was absolutely massive and covered with tough scales.

The knights, their senses confused, couldn't even grasp the monster's true location.

What will Captain Zackary do? Did he know how to fight a Green Nightmare? The Dream Bird only created illusions, but now the thing was all hard scales, sharp fangs, and deadly claws.

Like the Flower-Horned Deer, it normally stayed far from the forest edge, residing in the depths. Perhaps, back when I first called Zavilia here, I changed the monster's area of activity somehow?

Monster habitats always seemed to be changing. It even seemed like there were fewer monsters nowadays than there were three hundred years ago. Part of me wanted to believe it was because the demon lord was sealed away, but I needed more info. But if there *were* less monsters these days, I guess that could explain why nobody knew how to fight the Flower-Horned Deer and why Zackary so easily allowed the Dream Bird to transform into a Green Nightmare. Nobody who'd fought one before would ever make a mistake like that.

If Cyril were here, he'd be scolding everybody in sight. *I expect everybody to have read the monster list and already know how to fight it!* he'd say...but reality wasn't that simple.

I watched the mages move on Zackary's command, forming a line spanning east to west, then casting trap magic on the ground. It was basic trap magic that would cause an explosion when stepped on. So they were going to use it to figure out the Green Nightmare's true location, I figured? The knights stood five meters behind the trap magic, evenly spread out with their swords at the ready.

Paying no mind to the trap nor the knights, the Green Nightmare lunged forward with incredible speed...or so it seemed.

The knights tensed as the monster barreled fearlessly toward them. The vibration of the ground as it stepped, the smell of the earth as it kicked up dirt, the glint of its fangs and claws, and the fear heavy in the hearts of the knights—it was all too real. Before they knew it, the monster had stepped on the line of trap magic.

The knights rushed in to swing—but no explosion came.

The knights froze, confused. The lack of explosion meant that this Green Nightmare was an illusion. But the knights gave in and began striking vainly at the fake monster—their fear was stronger than their reason.

And right then, an explosion rocked the air...ten meters east of the illusion.

"What?!" The nearby knights, surprised, turned toward the source, but...

"Argh!"

"Gah!"

The knights were struck and knocked back another ten meters. The Green Nightmare had charged through diagonally. The knights had missed their one chance to grasp the monster's true location, and now things were just getting worse. At this point, they really might start accidentally hitting *each other*.

I clenched my fists. Knights went flying. Zackary stood still, gripping his sword tightly, powerless. He gritted his teeth in frustration, and I sighed. Could I really just "stay on the sidelines?" I glanced toward the familiars on standby. A few were already looking back at me.

The small unit I was in had five knights from the Fourth Monster Tamer Knight Brigade, accompanied by five familiars. Of those five familiars, three could fly—two C-rank eagle-type monsters and a D-rank owl-type monster.

"They're waiting for your orders, Fia. Their monster survival instinct tells them to help the one who healed them, in hopes that they may be healed once more someday as repayment. Even without a pact, they recognize you as their temporary master."

It didn't seem like Zavilia was wrong...the familiars had been staring at me for a while now. But would my orders get through to them without a contract? They couldn't read my thoughts without one. But then again, people often said that monsters had intuition far sharper than that of humans...

I pointed at the Green Nightmare, then raised my hand and pointed toward the sky above it. *Did I get through to them?*

I did indeed. The three familiars took flight the moment I pointed upward.

The illusion only worked under and within the circle the Dream Bird created. By having the familiars fly above the range of the illusion—ten meters high, in this case—they could indicate the true location to everyone.

The only problem was that the Green Nightmare could revert back to a Dream Bird, and way more quickly than it'd turned into a Green Nightmare. And a Dream Bird would have no trouble taking care of the C- and D-rank familiars above.

I raised a hand and whispered a spell. "Imprison all regardless of sin—Basic Prison!"

The spell was typically used to restrain enemies, but it could also be used like a cage to protect. This basic version of the spell would probably be enough to withstand a B-rank Dream Bird.

"Hide what must be hidden—Second-Class Shroud!" I cast

concealment magic after confirming the prison was made. "Heh heh!" I couldn't help but grin. "Now there's no way the Dream Bird can hit the familiars!"

Zavilia looked weary. **"Did you need to go that far? You're spoiling those familiars. If you're not careful, they'll become obsessed and start following you everywhere."**

"What?! I don't want that!" I said as the familiars arrived directly above the Green Nightmare. Being an A-rank monster, it had high intelligence and immediately caught on to what was happening. It transformed back into a Dream Bird and, with a single flap of its wings, drew near the familiars. It reached out its claws to scratch at the familiars but collided with something invisible in the air.

"What do you think, Zavilia?" I gloated. "An invisible barrier is *basically* an illusion, so I'm giving the Dream Bird a taste of its own medicine! Pretty cool, right?"

"Too bad you can't show it off to the other knights to hear what they think."

C'mon, Zavilia, can't you at least say it's cool?!

Still miffed, I called out. "Captain Zackary!"

He faced where he thought the Green Nightmare was and looked over at me.

"The Dream Bird is ten meters above you!" I shouted. "It's already left its own illusion range, so you should be able to see it! Tell the archers and mages to fire at it, and don't worry about hitting the familiars—they're ready to dodge! Have everyone withdraw while the Dream Bird is pinned down!"

Was that enough? I said a bit more, just in case. "The Dream Bird is outside its own illusion range right now, so now's the time to leave the circle it drew at the start and escape the illusions!"

Zackary looked at me with surprise, but he seemed to trust my words. He did what I said, and the knights managed to escape the illusion without further harm. Above them, an enraged Dream Bird and a few familiars soared about, all protected by an invisible cage.

"Now then," I said to the knights with a smile, "shall we take it from the top?"

You can't use inexperience as an excuse anymore, Zackary. Show me how you take down a Dream Bird properly this time!

Zackary saw me smiling and frowned. "F-Fia?!" he bellowed. "What's that devilish smile you're wearing?!"

"What are you talking about? I'm just a meek little recruit who's been staying on the sidelines just like you asked."

"Lies! What kind of meek little recruit *smiles* as they threaten a captain?! I can hear your tone. 'Oh, Zackary, I brought things back to square one for you. Better not screw it up this time'!"

"I thought no such thing. Sounds like an auditory hallucination! All I did was cheer you up with a smile!"

"You're just like this bald buff instructor I had in knight training school! He'd put us through the wringer every day with that sadistic smile of his, as though he were the demon lord himself!

I thought I'd die every lesson. Made it by the skin of my teeth! That chilling smile of yours...it's the same!"

"Did you really just compare me to some buff bald guy? Ha! Ha. Okay, sure. *Good luck!*"

I held my left hand in the air and lowered the strength of the concealment magic I cast, just enough for the cage around the familiars to become visible when viewed from directly below.

I'm not mad. I'm not! But there's only so much abuse I'm willing to take, even if it's from a captain. Besides, it's my magic! I can do what I want with it!

The Dream Bird gave up on attacking the familiars once it realized it couldn't reach them. It circled around, frustrated, before flying just below the cage and seeing what was obstructing it. When it found it couldn't break the spell, it let out an annoyed cry...and then made a beeline away from the familiars and toward the knights.

Freed from the illusions, the archers and mages fired at the Dream Bird again. They'd learned from earlier, blasting it with fire magic as it closed in—that'd been the most effective spell last time.

The Dream Bird wasn't such a big threat without its illusions. Its flight trajectory was hard to read, and though its attacks were nothing to scoff at, the knights knew how to deal with them now. Amazing.

However!

I still couldn't forgive Zackary for saying I was like some buff bald guy! I didn't hold a grudge for what he said—okay, I *did* hold a grudge—but we needed his strength. More than he was using now, actually. Sure, a commanding officer has a responsibility to observe everything, but it was keeping him from really going all out.

From the corner of my eye, I saw the Dream Bird descend erratically, trying to fly low enough to create the boundary for its illusionary space again. If you knew it needed to trace out the high and low points of its boundary to complete its illusion, you could potentially predict when and where it'd come low enough to strike. One hit from Zackary would probably finish it, but... he probably wouldn't predict its trajectory on his first time seeing it.

Jeez...I expect too much from Zackary just because he's a bit strong. It really would be best if we finished this quickly. Dream Birds *knew* they weren't that strong without illusions, so they often came with backup. Maybe we'd lucked out when it showed up alone, or maybe monsters were just scarcer these days.

But with the recent cases—

"Three new monsters, seven o'clock!" yelled a detection mage.

With the recent cases of monsters wandering outside their normal habitats, there was a fair chance we'd come across more creatures.

I stood between the saints and the incoming monsters and turned to my seven o'clock. Two boar-type monsters and a single deer-type monster pushed through the overgrown grass.

"T-two Violet Boars and one Flower-Horned Deer!" called the knight closest to them.

The Violet Boars were one thing, but the Flower-Horned Deer was B-rank—it was supposed to take around thirty knights to bring one down. To arrive while we were already fighting a different B-rank monster...

Nice timing! This'll be good training for everyone!

"There're two B-rank monsters..." a knight murmured. "We're screwed..."

Oh, quit exaggerating. Captain Zackary will figure something out. Worse comes to worst, we can call the other units! That's what I thought, at least, before I heard the emergency whistle go off to the east of us.

Which was where Vice-Captain Gideon's unit was. Were they calling for help? Then, suddenly, another whistle went off from the west...where Captain Quentin was. Seriously?! He needed help too?

"Ugh, what luck!" Zackary groaned. "Just how many monsters are gathered here? And we can't even get help from the others?"

It seemed weird, though. I mean, what monster would Quentin and Gideon even need help with? Quentin and company could definitely deal with anything B-rank and below. With enough time, Gideon would be able to as well. Besides, Quentin had a griffon with him, and that was an A-rank monster. If something was giving him trouble, it'd have to be higher than A-rank...

As though to confirm my suspicions, Zavilia said, "**Bad news, Fia. A dragon has appeared to the west. Two dragons.**"

"Uhh...dragons are S-rank, right? Doesn't it usually take about a hundred knights to bring 'em down? Feels like we're in a bit of a pickle."

"Well...I could probably deal with most dragons."

"Aw, aren't you something! What about the monsters on Vice-Captain Gideon's side? You know what they are?"

"Just one deer and one boar."

"A Flower-Horned Deer and a Violet Boar? Okay, he'll be fine. We can just leave him be!"

I turned to Zackary. "Captain! Vice-Captain Gideon's come across a Flower-Horned Deer and a Violet Boar!"

"Huh? H-how can you tell?!"

I ignored his question. "But we can't spare any men, so blow the whistle to tell them they're on their own!"

"R-right!" he agreed, though he looked confused.

"Two dragons have also appeared where Captain Quentin is! They definitely need our backup, so we should finish here quickly and head over!"

"D-dragons?! *Two* dragons?!"

"Two dragons! I think we should clear these monsters quick so we can help!"

"Hmph! There you go again, ordering us to do the impossible like it's nothing! You damn...buff bald instructor 2.0!"

Huh? I guess the stress of the situation was causing him to conflate my kind and humble advice with the orders of the devilish instructor he had in his student years.

I'll remember this, Captain Zackary, I thought, fuming. "Invigorate: Weight ×2!"

I cast the strengthening magic typically meant for myself or allies on the Dream Bird, but instead of making it stronger or faster, I increased its weight. It let out a surprised cry as its body weight doubled, and it started frantically flapping its wings...but it couldn't resist gravity. It struggled in the air but lost altitude with every beat of its wings. It slowly approached the ground, flapping wildly all the way.

Oh, shoot—I wasn't supposed to help. I'd planned to use this opportunity to teach the knights a lesson, but I was too worried about Quentin. Ah, well. At least I could let Zackary deal the final blow, right?

"Captain Zackary, we're short on time! Finish it in one strike, please!"

"You...slave driver!" Complaining all the while, Zackary ran full force at the Dream Bird, unsheathed his sword, and felled it in a single, powerful slash.

Huh. So Zackary wields a greatsword with two hands. Weird. Suits him, though.

The way he'd positioned himself before he struck...I couldn't help but smile at that. He'd quickly figured out the lowest point where the Dream Bird would pass and used that to strike. Zackary really was something after all!

"Wonderful job, Captain Zackary!" I said and pointed to the west. "Now, let's go support Captain Quentin! We can leave the rest of these monsters to the others!"

"Huh?! A-are you crazy, Fia?! We still have the B-rank Flower-Horned Deer left! It's not something these guys can handle alone!" Man, he really didn't want to abandon his men.

Hmm...I get where you're coming from, but the dragons are a way bigger threat. We should focus on helping Quentin...but I can't go against the words of the commanding officer, at least not directly...

My plan hadn't felt right, but I still turned to the remaining knights facing off against the Flower-Horned Deer and the Violet Boar. "Hey! You guys in the Sixth Knight Brigade studied how to take down Flower-Horned Deer, right?! Remember how you got to eat its meat thanks to me last time?! Why don't you guys put some work in and pay me back in meat?"

"Th-that's coercion..." I heard a single knight sputter back.

I pretended I didn't hear him. "Still, sometimes letting prey go is for the best. If you think its meat isn't fatty enough yet and want to let it go for next time, cut off its horn. Just a single piece breaking off will make it run away. Hitting its horn head-on should do the trick!"

"F-Fia, you kept that information from us last time on purpose, didn't you?!" a knight complained.

Another knight shook his head. "'Chubby Savior?' Y-you're more like a demon out of hell..."

The knights whispered in fear, but I just hung my head. Any monster that fought humans and survived would catch on to our tactics. Letting a monster go just meant we'd leave a smarter, deadlier monster for somebody else to deal with—*that's* why I hadn't told them about the horn last time. But I didn't have a choice.

Zackary could safely retreat to help Quentin and make it back in time to help with the Flower-Horned Deer and Violet Boar—I was sure of that, and sure that there wouldn't be casualties. But I couldn't convince Zackary to do so without making sure his guys weren't in too much danger. He cared deeply for his men. Of course, it wasn't impossible that new monsters might appear. Yeah, I could understand his worries, so I'd obey his orders.

An obedient recruit is a good recruit, after all! I thought to myself as I got ready to help.

But one of the knights suddenly spoke up. "Go! You can leave this to us, Fia!"

And another. "Yeah, we'll be fine! Work up an appetite for deer meat tonight, eh!"

A third. "Fighting this thing without the captain sounds scary, but we're not about to turn tail!"

"Guys?" I muttered, confused.

The knights seemed a little more gallant than usual as they faced the monsters.

I was overwhelmed with emotion. "H-how manly! Knights really are the coolest," I muttered. *Pull yourself together, Fia.* "You have some good men, Zackary! I'm sure we can leave this to them. Let's help Captain Quentin!"

"R-r-right!" Zackary stammered.

I turned back toward the knights one last time. "Everyone from the Fourth Monster Tamer Knight Brigade, dragons have appeared near Captain Quentin's unit! We're going to go help. Can you lend me your familiars?"

"D-dragons?! You're kidding...um, of course! Take them! Anything for the Captain!"

"You can take them, but they won't listen to you! We're their masters and they aren't even listening to *us*! They've just been flying around in the air!"

I ordered them to do that, actually—I thought, but it was probably better not to admit that.

"Thank you for your permission!" I released the barrier protecting the familiars. The three familiars that had been flying around and the two familiars waiting on the ground rushed toward me.

"Huh? What in the..."

"Wait...what?"

The knights sounded surprised, but I didn't have time to tell them anything—I had to run. Zavilia took to the air, making a beeline toward Quentin. He was the only one who could lead us to Quentin's precise location.

Behind me, the knights were getting pretty raucous.

"Wh-what *is* that girl? Some kind of legendary monster tamer?!"

"They're obeying her more than their own masters?! But she didn't even give them orders!"

I'm not sure what a legendary monster tamer is supposed to be, I thought to myself as I ran full speed ahead, *but it's a hundred times better than being called a buff bald guy!*

In a few minutes, a dizzying sight came into view: there really were two blue dragons, each around five meters tall. It was scary stuff—even from a distance, I felt a creeping despair at the sight of them.

I...don't think we can defeat them. We'd better retreat as soon as possible, but what do the captains think?

I quickly scanned the area, and there Quentin was. Things did *not* look good for him.

Why's Captain Quentin standing so close to the blue dragons? That's gotta be less than ten meters! I mean, you'd need nerves of steel to stand up to those things, so I can at least admire it. I would've definitely bolted off by now. Captain Quentin's really something else... I frowned thoughtfully. *I don't think I'll ever understand him.*

Zavilia swooped down and landed on my shoulder. **"Those two dragons are mates. They've probably come looking to stockpile food before breeding."** He sighed through his nostrils, exasperated. **"But that strange knight just keeps getting stranger..."**

You mean Quentin?

"He values monsters as much as humans. The man is fully prepared to lose his life to save his familiar."

You think so? I looked over to one of the dragons. It was pinning a griffon under one of its great claws. Quentin was facing the dragons head-on to save his familiar.

We've got some impressive captains, huh? Captain Zackary won't abandon a single subordinate, and Captain Quentin refuses to abandon his familiar. How wonderful!

"Hmph. 'Impressive' is one way to put it. These men have a duty to protect as many knights as they can. Endangering all for the sake of one is the height of stupidity."

"But it's not like they're throwing *everything* away to try to save one more. I'm sure Captain Quentin won't defeat the blue dragon, but I bet he can at least save the griffon." The captains weren't dumb. No, they'd begrudgingly abandon the few to save the majority if they really had no other choice. But until that moment came, they'd do all they could. That was the kind of captain I believed them both to be. That was why everyone trusted them so much.

"I really admire that about them," I said aloud.

Zavilia let out a weary sigh. **"For all of their talents, the way they risk their lives is what fascinates you? I cringe to think of your future love life."**

"Wha—Zavilia, don't jinx it!" Ugh, where was wood to knock on when you needed it? I furiously shook my head, as though that could shake off Zavilia's jinx, then reassessed the situation.

The griffon was still pinned by a five-meter-tall blue dragon, and a second blue dragon of similar size stood diagonally behind it. Quentin stood with Zackary, ten meters from the two dragons. Far behind the captains stood around fifteen knights and ten familiars. As for saints...I didn't see any, so they probably ran away.

Our odds weren't great. The two captains were strong, but we seriously lacked the manpower to take on two blue dragons. What could the two possibly be planning?

"Fia," Zavilia spoke up. **"Long ago, I too was a blue dragon."**

"Huh?!" I gave Zavilia a look, surprised. "Do you have memories of your past life like me?! Oh, wait...um, let's see. I remember now—after a dragon lives a thousand years, uhh..."

"After one thousand years, blue dragons are reborn as black dragons. That's how I came to be."

"Oh."

"I know it's asking a lot, but...Fia, I'd rather not fight blue dragons if possible," Zavilia whispered hesitantly.

Wow. Zavilia had never asked me not to do something before. What kind of friend would I be if I refused him?!

"O-of course, Zavilia! Just leave it to me!" If he used to be a blue dragon, then those two were something like distant relatives. Who *wouldn't* be reluctant to fight?

I smiled to try to reassure him, but he just hung his head sadly. **"Sorry, Fia."**

Oh no! Don't be sad, Zavilia! Ugh...if this goes sour, he'll feel so bad for not helping! I gotta do something!

At that instant, Quentin ran forward. I watched in awe as he drew his sword and leapt, swinging at the blue dragon pinning his griffon down. Zackary moved as well, swinging at the same dragon from the other side.

So fast! And strong too... I thought, wide-eyed. Zackary's dexterity with the greatsword was incredible! He didn't slow down once, maintaining momentum by turning his blade with perfect timing. He was clearly a master of the greatsword and must have possessed incredible muscle to swing it so long without tiring.

I watched in awe. Every few strikes, he made a particularly brutal one.

"Captain Zackary's incredible!" one of the knights cried. "He keeps landing critical hits!"

No, he's using Invigorate, I thought. It was imperfect, but he'd somehow learned Invigorate through combat experience alone. I felt unadulterated admiration for him. *Amazing...*

I'd never seen someone learn Invigorate all on their own, even imperfectly. His affinity for combat must've been tremendous—genius, even!

Quentin was strong too, moving in tandem with Zackary. He used his bastard sword freely, alternating between one-handed grip and two-handed seamlessly.

The blue dragon fought back, whipping its tail at the pair, but the captains evaded with ease. Filled with rage, the blue dragon inadvertently raised the foot pinning the griffon, giving just enough of an opening for the griffon to break free. *Heck yeah!*

Despite its injuries, the griffon flew toward Quentin, stopping in the air just behind him instead of fleeing.

S-so brave! I was practically moved to tears. Quentin must've showered his familiar with tons of love, and now his griffon was returning the favor. *Good for you, Captain Quentin! You found someone who loves you back! I mean, they're a monster, but still!*

The blue dragon was enraged at losing its prey. Worse yet, it could move freely now that it wasn't pinning anything down... and now the other dragon was finally taking interest in the fight.

As if they'd planned it, the two captains immediately began running my way.

"Retreat!" Quentin shouted. "Archers, mages, familiars, provide support! Everybody else retreat quickly, but don't lose sight of the blue dragons!"

The two captains rushed over to the knights before turning around and brandishing their swords at the blue dragons, ready to cover everyone's retreat. *Wow, these captains are real men!*

Not wanting to let their bravery go to waste, I ran full speed alongside the other knights. The familiars with me joined with their fellows, flying around the blue dragons, trying to draw their attention. The archers and mages stayed behind to provide support.

Just when I thought we might actually get away, one of the blue dragons looked to the sky and, with a flap of its wings, took to the air. The other followed.

Starting with the griffon, the winged familiars tried to obstruct its path, but nope—they were all knocked away. The dragons were just too huge.

The two blue dragons flew straight for us, rapidly closing the distance.

"Th-they're coming!" one of the knights cried in horror.

All at once they were here, and they quickly descended.

A small gap had formed between the retreating knights, and I could see now exactly which specific knight the blue dragons were aiming for.

Me.

Up in the boundless blue sky, a dragon fast approached with its maw wide and teeth glistening.

Oh no—I'm done for. My body tensed for what would come when a blue figure passed through my vision.

"Fiaaaaa!"

Captain Quentin? Captain Zackary? Faster than I could register the speaker, a blast of wind kicked up a cloud of dust in front of me. From within the billow of dust, a black figure towered.

"Oh...Zavilia!"

A large, beautiful, black monster had appeared to protect me... the legendary monster known as the black dragon.

A Tale of the
Secret
Saint

Zavilia, Black Dragon

"I SAW A DREAM of the past..." I muttered.

"Oh, Zavilia, you silly goose. What past? You're zero years old!" she laughed.

I was always happy with Fia...so happy, warm, and safe.

The stark difference between my life now and the many years of solitude I lived reaffirmed just how worthless those days long ago truly were.

Fia...the two millennia I've endured are nothing compared to my time with you...

◇ ◇ ◇

I was born a nameless blue dragon with a missing wing.

Dragons are born from eggs, and I was no exception. The only thing that was, perhaps, exceptional about my birth was that my egg had two yolks. In other words, I was a twin.

Humans often bore healthy twins, but dragons weren't so fortunate. Double-yolked eggs have complications, you see: the size of the egg doesn't change with the number of yolks, nor does the total amount of nutrients inside it. So, I thought to myself from within my egg: *How can I survive with only half the nutrients?*

The answer I arrived at was simple. I merely needed to stay small.

I kept my growth in check and stayed smaller than normal, somehow managing to survive until hatching.

My twin brother, however, did not.

He thoughtlessly grew, becoming as large as a normal baby dragon. At the rate he developed, he wouldn't have enough nutrients to survive until hatching.

And so...he ate my wing.

I still remember the morning I was born. It was spring. A heavy thunderstorm crackled outside the cave, as though rejoicing at our birth.

Our mother was already by our side when our shell hatched. She carefully peeled off the bits of shell that clung to my brother, who left the egg first, and then bestowed him a name. Names held power. By naming her son, she was granting a piece of her own power unto him.

The moment he was named, his body shone and grew double the size, and his pale-yellow skin changed to vivid blue.

I watched my brother with envy, spreading my one wing and sprawling my body flat onto the floor, waiting for my turn. You see, I still believed that my turn would come.

My mother took a single glance at my lone wing before turning away for good, taking my brother and leaving me behind in the cave.

Bits of shell stuck messily to my head and body; the base of my chewed-off wing throbbed and ached. Unnourished, I hungered. And still I waited.

I waited. I believed that my mother would return, would gently peel away the lingering bits of shell on my head and bestow a name upon me.

A day passed.

Then a second.

A third.

I sat still throughout, simply listening to the endless rain pouring outside the cave. That must be why I've always despised rain, despite the instinctual fondness dragons usually have for it. The sound of rain is akin to a worm slithering beneath my skin.

On that fateful day, I stepped out of the cave and into that abhorrent rain, all the while fighting against the wretched, skin-slithering sound.

The rain—sickeningly warm in the spring breeze—soaked me. But I had to keep moving. I could sense I was at my limit, that I would not survive another day without food, and…I finally understood that my mother would not return.

It was so simple. So logically sound. An injured baby dragon was not likely to survive until adulthood, so why take that chance when you already had another child?

All alone, I would have to survive with this stunted, disfigured body...this body deemed unworthy of even being given a name by the mother who birthed it.

How might others have seen me back then? I can only wonder.

There was no such thing as a dragon without a name, and there was no dragon so pale, so small. I couldn't even walk well due to the uneven weight of my single wing, much less fly.

But as ironic as it was, being so undragonlike helped me to survive. A name would've given me some of my mother's memories with her power. With it would have come the pride of a dragon, and such overwhelming pride would've kept me from drinking muddy water or scavenging the leftovers from other monsters. Because I didn't look like a dragon, other monsters did not question my actions.

By the time I had survived a full year, I was large enough to take on mid-level monsters...but, of course, my missing wing kept me from flight.

After yet another year, I finally found what I had been looking for—a flock of blue dragons. It had taken two years of searching, a reasonable length of time considering I was clueless where they might be. I found them deep in the forest where they had made their nesting grounds in a series of dim caves, a favorite habitat for dragons.

A young dragon on lookout warned me as I approached. But once they saw my pale yet still faintly blue skin, they welcomed me. Dragons formed flocks with those of the same species. Even a young stray like me would be welcomed, as long as I wasn't a problem.

There were around ten other blue dragons in the flock. The chief was a remarkably large dragon with a scar above their right eye.

As for my mother and brother...I did not find them there, although I also did not care. I'd lived my entire life without them, after all. I simply wanted the comfort of living with my own kind.

I spent ten years there. My light color and lack of a wing earned me ridicule from the others but never caused me any larger problems. Ridicule was nothing compared to the comfort of knowing that I had a place to sleep, food to eat, and my kind by my side. Even being at the bottom of the male hierarchy didn't bother me, although it did mean I was sent on every hunt. But this turned out to be a blessing in disguise, as I gained much combat experience and quickly got stronger.

Within a decade, I was the second strongest dragon after our chief. The others acknowledged my strength and started calling for me when they needed help in battle. Naturally, I was simply happy to be needed. Happy to help my flock. Never once did the idea of fighting other males to improve my social standing occur to me.

We lived our days in peace, until one night a pack of fenrir attacked. Fenrir were powerful gray-wolf-like monsters that hunted in packs of ten or so. On that night, though, they numbered more than twenty—their leader was surely mighty. They attacked in our sleep. We were easily surrounded and outnumbered.

With a skyward roar, our chief called on us to abandon our nests. All the blue dragons who heard it took to the air, one after another. The only ones left on the ground were my flightless self, our chief—who roared and roared—and a single blue dragon who was attacked by the fenrir before they could fly off.

But the chief underestimated the fenrir; he should have waited until he was airborne before giving the signal to abandon the nests. The fenrir leapt at him as he roared, piling onto him relentlessly. Before I knew it, he'd collapsed to the ground, covered by fenrir.

I rushed to the chief's side and tore away the fenrir clinging to him. I was stronger now—strong enough to make up for not having a wing, strong enough to rip the throats of my enemies, strong enough to tear limb from limb—but there were simply too many.

By the time I tore away the last fenrir, the chief was barely breathing. He clearly had little time left.

I bent down to hear his last words when the unexpected happened—the chief gave me his blessing. For the first time in the twelve years I'd lived, I was blessed. Warmth filled my body as it began to glow.

In his final moments, he entrusted me his name and power. It was only possible because I was nameless.

What a coincidence that I, the nameless dragon, should be by his side in his final moments. But it was by that very coincidence that *I* came to be.

I, Zavilia.

The moment I was named, my body took on a deep-blue color. I grew in size and sprouted again the wing I had lost before my birth.

I soared, flying high enough that the fenrir below looked like nothing more than wisps of grain.

Ah...I still recall my first flight. Oh, what a sublime feeling...

"Grooooooah!" I unleashed a deep, triumphant roar before rapidly descending straight toward the lone dragon that had been attacked before they could take flight.

Soon enough, I realized that I'd overestimated my strength. The sudden rush of strength I felt as the chief's power became my own only made me *think* I was invincible...but that false confidence turned out to be a blessing.

Fenrir and blue dragons were usually equal in strength, so it was common sense to never fight more than one at a time. But common sense was nothing to me! I flew into the pack of fenrir alone. They were intelligent monsters with sharp intuition, but my abnormal confidence overwhelmed them. I could've never truly bested the ten-some fenrir present, but intimidating them was enough. The fenrir loosened their bite on the blue dragon just long enough that the dragon could slip away and take flight.

With my last ally freed, I had no reason to stay at our old nesting grounds. I took to the skies once again.

"Graooooo!" I roared and flew to the east.

My fellow dragons understood that I had inherited the chief's power. Until then, they'd been gazing blankly at the chief's lifeless body, but finally they followed after me.

I was flying to the cave I was born in, the only safe place I could envision.

When I arrived, an unfamiliar blue dragon was there. Seeing me and my flock land, the blue dragon said something...and another dragon appeared from within the cave.

It was my brother. He had grown into a splendid adult dragon, and he was now the chief of a flock of five. My mother stood behind him.

Being first, the cave was rightfully theirs, but they allowed us to stay in a part of the cave.

With the old chief's power, I succeeded him. It was now my responsibility to ensure the flock's peace and safety. There was no doubt in my mind I could do it with my unparalleled strength and my two proper wings. Ten years ago, my flock had accepted my feeble self. It was time to repay that debt. I swore to myself I would protect everyone, no matter how young or weak they were. Such an ideal seemed natural to one such as me, who had struggled so much.

I wanted to try talking to my brother, hoping that we could work together to protect our flocks, but he avoided me at every turn. He may have eaten my wing, but I bore no ill will over it. Prioritizing one's own life was simply the nature of monsters, and—being a monster—I could hardly fault him. My mother avoided me as well, never leaving her own cave chamber when I was around.

For a time, we seemed to flourish. Our flock had small quarrels here and there, but nothing major, and there was always enough prey to hunt. We were attacked by other monsters count-less times, but I alone was enough to fend them off.

As I used it, I grew more accustomed to my newfound strength, becoming even more powerful. And I was happy! No monster would hate being strong, but it was more than that—the joy of my strength came from knowing that I could protect my flock. I believed that my flock felt the same way, knowing they were safe.

If there was anything that I thought could be a problem then, it was living space. Things were cramped with two flocks, so I began to leave the cave at times to search for a new place we could nest.

One night, everything changed. A fierce storm raged outside of our cave, blotting out the moon. I was asleep when I felt it, that sharp pain on my neck. It was my brother biting down on me, with his flock waiting behind him.

I could beat my brother alone, but I could not beat all five of them.

His actions surprised me. I could understand him challeng-ing me to a duel in an attempt to seize leadership over my flock, but a surprise attack like this? It wasn't how dragons did things. I had been wary since the fenrir attack and increased the number of lookouts, but I'd never once expected an attack from inside the cave.

My brother glared at me with his maw clamped down on my neck. <Just eating your wing in that egg was a mistake!> he snarled, his voice dripping with malice. <I should have eaten you whole then! That power is rightfully mine... You stole it from me!>

I fought the pain as I tried to understand my brother's crazed words. What was he talking about? Eating me wouldn't give him my strength. If such a thing were possible, we'd have all killed each other long ago.

<Brother, please calm down.> I had never called him "Brother" before. <My power won't pass on to you even if you eat me. We're brothers; we should be working together instead of fighting.>

<You were just some stunted, one-winged piece of trash back then!> he roared. <I figured eating you whole would just make me weaker...so how are you like this now?! Did you really deceive your chief and take his power, boasting as if it were your own?! You're vile—the vilest dragon I've ever laid eyes on!> He cursed and raged, never once loosening his grip.

The time for words was finished. I pulled my neck from his hold, willingly shedding some skin and flesh, and ran out the cave, leaving my brother and his flock behind. My flock outnumbered his; I should be fine as long as they noticed what was happening.

That was when I saw the dragons encircling the entrance to my cave. A flash of lightning illuminated their figures in the dark... the figures of my own flock.

Why are they here? Did they come to help when they heard the fight? My mind raced as I stood stock-still, confused. That was when they spoke.

<I've always hated you for stealing our chief's power and lording over us! Know your place!>

<Who do you think you are to order us around when you used to be such weak trash?!>

<You planned to steal the chief's power the whole time, didn't you? You pale, one-winged freak!>

What in the world are they saying? I thought. *If you all felt that way, why didn't you help our chief when he was attacked? Then maybe one of you would be chief instead...*

But I knew why, just as they did: they were too weak to do anything but watch our chief die from the air.

I was grasping at straws now. <If you were all so dissatisfied with me as chief, why didn't any of you duel me for the position? We can duel now if you'd like... We can settle this honorably.>

<Why should we show honor to a thief?!> they roared. <You should die a meaningless death, not even knowing who killed you!>

Yes...I understood now. They couldn't beat me in proper one-on-one combat. But by claiming that I was dishonorable, they could do away with rules and gang up on me without tarnishing their pride.

I looked around again at the faces of the dragons surrounding me.

I met the eyes of each female. *I understand how the males feel, but what of the females? Am I truly unwanted by everyone?* But each one averted her gaze.

<Sorry...but if you beat all the males, we'll be your mates,> said one.

<Thanks, but I only need one mate.> What strange dragons.

The males were willing to bend their pride till it snapped just to kill me, and the females—who clearly believed I wouldn't survive—were tacitly consenting to the actions of the males.

They were all so selfish, all only following the rules they wished to.

Was I deluding myself thinking they had accepted me? Was the debt I felt I owed them ever real? Or did they only see me as a convenient tool, a fighter who didn't talk back?

Was I...ever truly one of them?

I stared them down stoically. There was no mistaking it...I was on my own. The females wouldn't attack me themselves, I suspected, but they wouldn't help me either.

There's no way I can win. I...have to run. I was reluctant to fight. They had been my flock for ten years. I still couldn't shake the feeling that my strength existed to protect them.

As I hesitated, the males roared.

Graooooh!

Gieeeeee!

One of them leapt forward and bit into my arm.

I felt strangely calm. A flash of lightning illuminated the face of the dragon biting me, revealing a visage touched by madness but still unmistakably self-possessed. That was when I knew: they understood what they were doing and what their actions would bring.

There was no longer a reason to stay. My flock had no need for my protection.

I whipped my tail, sending the dragon biting my arm flying, and looked to the heavens above. The sickening, lukewarm rain poured down on me, coiling into my skin like a snake.

It's raining again. Why do bad things always happen on rainy days?

With a single flap of my wings, I flew high into the sky. In a mere instant, I was high enough to make my old flock appear as nothing more than wisps of grain. I looked at them for what would be the last time and roared.

"Grooooooah!" *Thank you and goodbye. I wish you all the best.*

Ten long years together had ended in but a moment. And yet none of us, not even I, lamented our parting.

I was a monster. My attachment to my flock was light. I felt nothing as I left the ones I had been with for ten years.

Nothing, just as when my twin brother and my mother left me long ago.

Nothing, just as when I was betrayed by my own flock.

Nothing. I would never see them again, and I felt nothing...

I flew north. At the northernmost tip of the continent was Blackpeak Mountain, where the most savage of monsters made their home. Freed from my flock, I could imagine no better place to live.

When I reached Blackpeak Mountain, I lived there for close to a thousand years. A blue dragon's life span was usually five hundred years at most, so I must have gained the time the previous chief was meant to live when I received his power.

The end approached as I neared my thousandth year...I could feel it. But in my final moments, the most unexpected thing happened: *I gave birth to myself.*

I gave birth to something so small and feeble, yet so beautiful and...black. Yes, black. Said to only exist in legend, it was a black dragon.

I faintly recalled hearing something about this back when I still lived in a flock.

"Any dragon who lives for a thousand years becomes a black dragon."

I had written it off as some fairy tale, but to think that it was true...

I was still in a daze, my blue dragon self having just bestowed upon me my name, my memories, and my power. My memories were still hazy. I felt like I was in a dream, but the power surging through my body was unmistakable.

Ha ha...incredible. Black dragons are truly this strong...

Black dragons were an ancient race of calamity-class monsters, so different from other dragons that they were hardly considered the same species. Now I was one of them.

I fully matured a year later. My body became incomparably stronger even compared to my infant form. A single flick of my tail was enough to deal with most monsters.

My strength was overwhelming, absolute.

And I needed no one.

I made my nest in Blackpeak Mountain's deepest cave and spent most of my time there, alone. I liked that cave; from there, I could not hear the rain, and no one was foolish enough to bother me.

I passed the next thousand years without meeting anyone, ruling comfortably over my kingdom of one.

Death came once again, and I was reborn as a small, feeble black dragon.

I looked up at an immense black dragon corpse, fallen onto its side like a great oak tree covered in moss.

And so begins another unchanging thousand years...

In the haze of rebirth, both my memories and power still hadn't taken root. I decided it'd be best to sleep for the time being, and I curled up into a ball.

Weeks passed until one day I woke, sensing a hostile presence. I found myself surrounded by countless yellow eyes peering at me from the dark.

Hmm...I might be in a bit of trouble.

I rose slowly. My cave had plenty of exits prepared for emergencies, but each exit was blocked to me.

Ah, fenrir! I just can't seem to catch a break with these accursed fenrir...

A weary sigh escaped me. Some time ago, the territories of all monsters became set in stone, established around the continent's

Three Great Beasts. One of those Three Great Beasts was me, the black dragon, and another was the Black Fenrir, a higher sort of fenrir. Surrounding me now was the Black Fenrir's pack.

Among the yellow eyes peering at me was a single pair of red eyes. From their presence alone, I knew they were a cut above the rest.

Damn...you aimed for the one time in a thousand years I would be vulnerable.

I roared before they could lunge. **"Graooooo!"**

The fenrir flinched, giving me an opening to run for it. I chose to charge through their circle to my left—it'd be suicide to directly charge toward the Black Fenrir straight ahead, but I also expected a trap to be waiting directly behind me. Truth be told, I expected a trap to be waiting no matter *where* I went, but I'd seize even the smallest advantage I could find.

Teeth sunk into my shoulders, my legs, my wings, but I had no time to shake them off. If I stopped now, I'd be pulled down and killed.

Dragging along who knows how many fenrir, I ran and ran and *ran* through the pitch-black cave. The fenrir clamped hard with their teeth, occasionally falling off, alongside bits of my flesh.

I was bloody all over by the time I reached the exit of the cave and used the last of my strength to flap my wings.

Southwest...I have to go southwest...

I don't know why I thought that at that time, but it rose to mind clearly, like a guiding beam of light in the darkness.

It took everything I had to continue flapping my wings.

I have to go...have to go as far as I can...

I flew southwest, beyond the sight of the fenrir.

One of my wings was in terrible shape, making it difficult to fly straight, and I could no longer feel my legs after my furious dash. My tail was gone past the base. My consciousness was dim as well, fading from the blood loss. I don't know how many times I blacked out... Each time, the pain of falling through the trees shocked me awake.

Eventually, I reached the limit of my stamina and fell like an anchor straight into the forest.

No...I was so close...

My consciousness was faint as I fell, but I clearly remember my body growing smaller. Once again, I was an infant...and completely helpless.

Pain assailed my body as I slammed into the earth. Lukewarm rain drizzled down from above.

Of course it's raining...it always rains when bad things happen. Can't I at least be free of this rain in my last moments?

As a monster, I instinctually fought to survive, reverting my body to its infant form to conserve energy and focus on recovering. But I couldn't recover fast enough.

I'm done for. Regret overwhelmed me. I could feel my consciousness fading. *Damn. To think a black dragon like me was done in by another monster...*

There was no greater humiliation than to die by the hands of another monster. This was true as a blue dragon, and it remained true as a black dragon.

So, in the end, I die as I was born. Alone—

My consciousness cut off there.

When I next opened my eyes, a human was staring at me—a young girl with golden eyes and red hair. I looked at her dimly as she fed me something and spoke in a soothing voice. "It'll be okay."

What did she just feed me? I thought, only half-conscious. The liquid spread through my body, and then...then came the rush of pain.

Poison. She fed me poison!

With the last of my strength, I returned to my original size to defend myself. No black dragon would allow themselves the disgrace of dying to such underhanded means. I roared and tore into the girl's shoulder. Into her side. The girl didn't resist in the slightest.

How weak! Did she plan to throw her life away to kill me? I wondered...and then, suddenly, she smiled back as though she found the whole situation amusing.

Her hand moved slightly, then emitted light. The light entered my body and, in a single moment, healed me completely, leaving no trace of injury.

Wh-what?

My torn-up wing had been restored, my tail had regrown, and the wounds on my body were no more. I wondered how this could be...and in that instant, she showed me how. She began to restore her shoulder and flank before my eyes.

Oh. She's...a saint.

I was in awe. This girl had brought me from the edge of death just moments before my two-thousand-year life was lost. And this girl clearly shared her blessings with all, using her power to stave off the inescapable fate of death.

The realization made me tremble.

I wanted her power. I wanted to serve her, to stay by her side and continue receiving her blessings. Only then could I be free from that one, dark absolute of this world. Free from death!

I now understood why I went southwest after being attacked by the fenrir. I was looking for her, the only one who could save me.

I, a noble, proud black dragon, would never form a pact with one weaker than myself...and yet it only took moments for me to wish to serve her. I couldn't even begin to fathom how grand her saint powers must be.

Unaware of my ulterior motives, she willingly formed a pact of servitude with me. I found it strange how one could be so powerful and yet so careless. It was as though she did not understand that the pact meant we were connected, as if she did not care to check just who she was making the pact with.

That night, monsters appeared one after another. The scent of the girl's...the scent of *Fia's* blood lured them, but I dealt with them effortlessly. After the thirtieth appeared, however, I found myself bewildered by just how many monsters she was drawing in.

The last monster I defeated was an A-rank. Such a monster should only live in the deep recesses of the forest, which meant that Fia's smell was strong enough to draw in monsters from that far away...

When the girl woke, she asked something peculiar. "Um, about me being a saint...could you keep that a secret?"

Why? I thought. *The world would worship you if they knew your power.*

She looked at me sadly and trembled. "I...I was killed in my past life because I was a saint. I don't want that to happen again."

Through our connection, I felt her emotions and even saw the memory she was thinking of. It was a sight no young girl should ever have to endure.

How terrible...

"By your will, I will keep your secret," I said sincerely. **"I'll always do what I can to protect you."**

She seemed embarrassed as she averted her eyes and blushed. I wasn't exactly fond of people, having lived alone for all these years, and yet I found myself worried about her.

What's with this saint? It's as if she's completely oblivious to the ways of the world. If left alone, she would just be used...

From then on, I watched over Fia both from a distance and from her side. She never ceased to surprise me, always getting into deeper trouble than I could've possibly imagined. It was a wonder she still hadn't been outed as a saint, and yet I also understood why: she was simply too fantastical! She so exceeded everyone's understanding of what was possible that none even considered that she might be a saint.

Monsters and humans didn't have much in common, but they

both liked to gossip. As far as I had gathered, there had only been one person known as "the Great Saint" in the past two thousand years. Surely, Fia understood the significance of that.

Just recently—and on a whim!—she turned an entire spring into healing potion as easily as if she were playing in a puddle. And not just any healing potion, mind you, but an ancient, superior variety lost to time. Even now, the spring churns out more of that mighty potion.

Fia was probably the most important person in the world... and yet no one knew it. Even *she* did not know it.

"*Ta-da!* Your very own disguise!" The most important person in the world wasted her time doing mundane things for me.

"Zavilia, you're suuuch a cutie!" she said, smiling as she stroked my head. She even let me sleep snuggled up against her warm body.

Sometimes I dreamt of the past, of the two thousand years I spent alone.

"Oh, Zavilia, you silly goose. What past? You're zero years old!" she laughed. That was when it came to me. I finally understood *why* I'd felt nothing on that night.

My flock thought nothing of me, and thus their betrayal had meant nothing. Thus I *felt* nothing as we parted.

But Fia was different. I'd give my life for her in a heartbeat because I knew she would never betray me. She accepted all of me for who I was. She got angry for my sake. She fought for my sake. She was always there to laugh with me.

I was always happy, warm, and safe with Fia. The stark difference between my life now and my many years of solitude reaffirmed just how worthless those days were, and, in turn, reminded me just how precious my time with Fia was.

I wouldn't give up my time with her for the world. So when those two blue dragons swooped down on her, I felt my blood boil over with rage.

Without hesitation, I flew before Fia and transformed into a black dragon, creating a gust of air that kicked up dust. I roared at the blue dragons as they rapidly descended, then flew up to meet them. They pulled away and rose back into the air. Just when I thought they would flee, they paused, stalling high above. The difference in our levels of strength should've been clear, and yet they seemed unwilling to leave.

Hmph. Again, huh?

I sighed, exasperated that Fia kept drawing in monsters like this. Thinking back on it, she had used her healing magic on the familiars earlier this morning. With her high tolerance for pain, she probably hadn't even noticed some minor injury. And so the sweet scent of her saint blood spread far into the air as she healed. That would explain the unusually high monster appearance rate. Everyone thought the monsters were wandering outside their normal habitats because of my appearance, but that alone wouldn't explain why so many powerful monsters appeared so close to the entrance, one after another.

Still unaware she was attracting all these monsters, Fia reached out and patted me. "Thank you for protecting me, Zavilia. You can leave the rest to me and the knights."

She still respected my selfish request to not fight the blue dragons. I couldn't help but laugh. So strange and foolish was this saint, and yet so sweet.

Despite wishing so badly to conceal her sainthood, she didn't hesitate one moment to use her powers once the knights were in mortal danger. To her, another's peril was enough to make her forget her own. It confounded me to think that she, the most important person in the world, could risk her life so willingly for the sake of these insignificant, replaceable knights—especially when she was so fragile herself.

For her sake, I needed to become the Dragon King.

I needed to become somebody who could protect this fragile girl from the cruel world.

A Tale of the
Secret Saint

22
The Search for the
Black Dragon Part 2

ASHAMED, I looked up at Zavilia.

He glared at the two blue dragons above us and let out a roar. I immediately created a barrier with my magic to protect the knights from the sound, sure that things wouldn't be pretty if they heard. The two blue dragons didn't retreat. They just bared their fangs threateningly.

Zavilia... He said that he didn't want to fight blue dragons because he used to be one. What kind of friend would I be if I couldn't grant his one request?

I patted him on the back. "Thank you for protecting me, Zavilia. You can leave the rest to me and the knights."

I turned around to face those knights, only to find almost all of them making the same face—wide-eyed and mouth agape.

"I-Is that the B-B-B-B-Black...Dragon...King?!"

"N-n-n-no way...th-the legendary ancient dragon is *real*?!"

They looked at me in horror.

"F-F-F-Fia!" a knight yelled. "Q-q-quickly! Run!"

"Y-yeah, run! B-before it kills you!"

Only Quentin wore a different expression. He seemed overcome with emotion, hands clasped in front of him as he stared at Zavilia, spellbound.

"Such a...a sublime form! Oh, how lucky am I to gaze upon you in all your majesty! Your splendor...your divine beauty! No...no words can do thee justice!"

Yeah...I guess I'm used to him being a weirdo now, huh?

A single knight started laughing hysterically. "I—ha—I think the fear's getting to me! I'm starting to see and hear things. I could swear I just heard Fia talk to the Black Dragon King and even call it by name! Crazy! Like it was her friend or something! Hell, I even saw her pat its back. I'm losing it for sure!"

Yeah, everyone's panicking. They probably won't notice if I cast a little strengthening magic on them!

I extended my hands toward the knights...but before I could cast my strengthening magic, Zavilia pressed his head against my back. Surprised by this sudden display of affection, I turned around to look at him. "Zavilia?"

"Thank you for taking my grumblings seriously. I was...confused. I lost sight of what was really important to me." He looked up at the blue dragons above. **"Leave those two to me, Fia. I had my priorities backwards when I said I didn't want to fight blue dragons. Above all, I wish to protect you."**

I didn't have time to reply. He soared into the air with his grand wings and, with but a few flaps of them, he flew higher than those blue dragons. Alarmed by his speedy approach, the two blue dragons spread out beneath him, baring their teeth in an attempt at intimidation, surrounding him on either side.

I looked up at the three dragons and gulped. *Is this all right? Zavilia's strong, but it's two on one...*

The two blue dragons were mates and probably knew how to fight together, and Zavilia had only matured recently. Could his fangs really pierce their hard scales?

I couldn't stop worrying about him. Then he suddenly descended, as if he didn't care that he was surrounded. Utterly unfazed by their intimidation, Zavilia swerved toward one and effortlessly sunk his fangs into the base of its neck. The blue dragon couldn't even react.

"Huh?" From below, I could've sworn that Zavilia looked pained as he sunk his teeth into the dragon's neck. But he bit the blue dragon's neck in two, and the pieces fell dead to the earth.

"Ah—move it!" a knight shouted. They all hurried to avoid the falling corpse. The two pieces of the blue dragon crashed with a deafening thud right where the knights had stood moments prior. A great cloud of dust erupted from the collision. Knights went flying. Sprawled on the ground, the knights looked up at Zavilia in sheer terror.

"Wh-wh-wh-what is that thing?"

"Th-the Black Dragon King is this strong?"

"Death itself! *It's death itself!*"

The knights watched in horror as the remaining blue dragon, enraged by the death of its mate, charged Zavilia. It roared and swooped up...and was sent flying with a swing of Zavilia's tail.

Zavilia faced the blue dragon and opened his maw to roar. The sound-blocking barrier I'd set up protected everyone from that roar, but not the shock wave that came after. I tensed in anticipation of the ear-splitting roar, but what came next...was dragonfire. The fire bore straight through the blue dragon's neck and down into the forest below, blazing a swath of it black. The blue dragon fell just as its companion had, crashing to the earth with a resounding thud.

"Uh..." No proper words formed in my mouth. I could only flap my jaw open and shut like a beached bass. This was my first time seeing Zavilia fight, and he was stronger than I could have ever imagined.

Wh-what? Zavilia's this strong? That baby dragon, Zavilia... that child...will he get even stronger?!

The other knights looked just as stunned, their faces frozen stiff with shock.

Everyone watched as Zavilia gracefully descended to me. He straightened his back and met my eyes silently. Still shocked, I managed to look up, wanting to thank him...and then I noticed something strange about his appearance.

"Uh...Zavilia, did you always have that horn?"

A splendid horn sprouted from the middle of Zavilia's forehead now. It hadn't been there before...had it?

"**Fia...**" His voice was filled with determination. "**I shall now become a king.**"

"Huh?" I couldn't hide my surprise. "A...king?" *The Black Dragon King...is this why everyone calls him that?*

Zavilia nodded. "If I stay as I am, fighting alone, I'll one day lose to the many roving groups of monsters. That's why I must become the Dragon King. I must rule over my people—over my dragons."

"Uh...yeah. Yeah, okay, go for it...?" *Didn't he say something about becoming a king before? I'll support him if this is what he wants...but I'll really miss him.*

"Fia, black dragons grow three horns when they become king. I've never wanted to become king—in fact, I never knew how I would *become* a king—but this horn grew when I protected you. Yes...just as a king cannot exist without subjects, I now know that I must protect many dragons to become worthy of having three horns."

He chuckled lightly. "I don't think I can keep up with you as I am now." He raised his front leg, then... "So let me go become someone who can protect you."

And Zavilia, the black dragon, snapped his own horn off.

"Huh?!" I exclaimed. His horn, as tall as a grown man, toppled from his head and pierced the ground upright. "Wh-what?! But you just got it! Why'd you—"

My voice was drowned out by Quentin's scream. "Th-the Black Dragon King's horn has broken! *Aaaaaaaaaaaaah!*"

Zavilia glared at Quentin and Zackary and, in a low, threatening tone, spoke. "Protect Fia until I return...and if you fail to offer your very *life* to her, I may take it!" His massive legs kicked his own broken horn to the captains. "Behold your payment! May you use this to protect Fia instead of your dull swords."

"Th-the Black Dragon King's horn?!" Quentin exclaimed, overtaken by awe. "Yes! I swear I'll protect Miss Fia, even at the cost of my own life!"

Uh. It was a little distasteful how ready Quentin was to risk his life when presented with Zavilia's horn, you know? "C-Captain Quentin, wait! Please think this over! A promise with a monster becomes an unbreakable contract once you agree to it!"

"Don't worry, Miss Fia!" he cried. "I'd do *anything* for the Black Dragon King's horn!"

"I-Is that right...?" Yeah, I wasn't gonna be able to talk him out of it...

Zavilia lowered his head. He was close to my face now, and his eyes—gravely serious—flitted to me. **"Our lives are connected. If something bad happens to you, I'll be the one to die first."**

"Huh?! Really?!"

Zavilia chuckled. **"Really. But I still want to do all kinds of things with you. Don't go too crazy while I'm gone, okay?"**

"I won't! I absolutely won't!"

"Ha ha...I think you will. Call it a hunch, eh? But that's all right. Be yourself, Fia. If anything happens, call for me. I'll come running." He winked at me playfully. **"Or flying, perhaps. Regardless, I'll be back before you know it, so...see you."**

I understood he was trying to keep things light by joking around, but...it was the way he said *"see you."* His voice, it was so dang small. I couldn't help but feel emotional.

"Zavilia..." I tried to sound happy. My voice cracked.

Zavilia...things are different from last time, when we had only known each other for a day. I won't forget you. No matter how many years pass.

I put my hands on his head and touched my forehead to his. "Okay. I love you, Zavilia. I'll be waiting for you to come home."

Having both said what we wanted, he left. With one beat of his great wings, Zavilia took to the skies.

By the time I remembered the plan we'd concocted at the meeting, Zavilia was already out of sight. "Ah! C-Captain Quentin, the rock, the rock! Throw the rock you got from Blackpeak Mountain!"

Snap, back to reality! Quentin threw the rock toward the direction Zavilia flew off to—but oh, there went gravity, and the rock skipped over the dirt uselessly. It was far too late.

"W-well, the order's wrong," I muttered, "but, hey...at least we did all the steps." And nobody said a word.

Everyone faced the direction Zavilia had gone with a look of blank awe on their faces. I couldn't blame them, really. Zavilia was just that amazing, you know? I could only follow suit and look the same direction.

Zavilia must've been looking at the same sky. Surely he was.

He was a black dragon—one of a beautiful, terrifying, legendary, ancient race of dragons, strong enough to defeat blue dragons with ease and proud enough to strive for the title of king. But he was also spoiled, a sleepyhead, easily jealous, oh-so-cynical...and someone I knew I could count on.

My dear friend, Zavilia.

I'll be waiting for you, bluebird. Come back, okay? Come back soon...

The Search for the Black Dragon Concludes

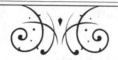

HE'S REALLY GONE...

Half-dazed, I gazed into the northern skies that Zavilia had flown into, as did the other knights around me. In that shocked fog, I wondered if we'd stay like this forever.

Zackary was the first to return to his senses. "Everyone, pull yourselves together!"

What a captain. Not only is he the first one back on his feet, but his first instinct is to help his subordinates get back on theirs. I looked at Zackary with admiration as he continued, his voice booming.

"Listen carefully! The shock of seeing the Black Dragon King has confused you all greatly! Everything you've seen, everything you've heard...consider it all the product of hallucinations brought on by fear!"

My look of admiration turned to worry. *Huh? What in the world is he on about? Are you sure you're not the confused one, Captain Zackary?*

Zackary returned my worried gaze with one of his own. "Especially you, Fia! Whether or not you know it, you're utterly losing it!"

"H-huh?! M-me?!" I blurted. Why was he singling me out?!

W-wait...I'm the one losing it? Oh gosh, I feel fine, but how can I know for sure? N-no, that can't be! Yeah! No way, right? My mind raced as I shot a smile at the other knights, looking for reaffirmation.

They simply shook their heads gravely. "Y-yes...yes, that must be it! You're just terribly confused right now...right? You have to be..."

"R-Right! Fia's a normal person...she's...normal...she *is* normal, right?"

The two knights trailed off into babbling that I couldn't quite make out. Whatever they were saying, it seemed like they all agreed with Zackary's words.

I took the words to heart. "Huh? Then I'm really losing it right now?!" I said frantically.

If I'm losing it, how do I get back to normal?! I looked back at Zackary for help, but he'd already moved on to addressing the other knights.

"Do not busy yourselves worrying about what was real and what was delusion—I will determine that later. For now, do *not* discuss anything that you saw or heard—or rather, that you *thought* you saw or heard. Are we clear?!"

"Yes, sir!" Everyone but me replied in unison.

Everything's happening too fast! O-oh no, I really am *losing it!*

My face paled, but Zackary seemed quite pleased with everyone's reply.

His face stiffened again, though, as he gave new orders. "Now, then—you three on the right, go look for the saints who fled into the forest! The rest of you split into two groups and join up with my unit and Gideon's! They're likely still fighting monsters, so be careful! Fia, you're with me!"

Though I was still concerned about my mental state, I went east with Zackary. After running behind him for a few minutes, we met up with the unit we'd left behind earlier. I couldn't see any monsters around, but everyone was frozen stiff and staring blankly to the sky.

H-huh? Wow, everyone's doing the whole blank-look thing here too. Guess it's a good day to zone out?

The unit leader came running up to Zackary. "C-Captain, you're back!"

"Yeah. A little late though, it seems." Zackary looked around. "Casualties?"

"Some injured, sir, but no casualties!"

Zackary breathed a sigh of relief. "And the monsters? There should be more corpses here."

There was only a single Flower-Horned Deer corpse.

"About that, sir! The Black Dragon King appeared a ways to the west just moments ago! Everyone, even the monsters, stopped to watch it fight in the air...and when it took down those blue dragons, the monsters just scurried off back into the forest!"

"Oh…" Zackary muttered. "So you could see that from here? Yes, I suppose they *would* run away after seeing that…"

The unit leader breathed a sigh of relief. "Thank goodness you're safe, Captain! I was worried for you when I saw those two blue dragons up there, but then the Black Dragon King appeared as well! A-ah, don't tell me…Captain Zackary, you fought against the Black Dragon King?! You really are amazing!"

He grabbed Zackary's hands and shook them, ecstatic. But eventually the handshake turned into a trembling grip.

"Th-that monster," he said, "is death itself. The moment I saw it kill the blue dragons, I thought it was going to come for us next. But I couldn't run! None of us could! We just stood there, staring. In the end, it didn't so much as glance at us. It flew north, sparing us as if on a whim…"

Zackary swallowed. "Yeah." His tone changed suddenly. "All right, everyone, listen up! The appearance of the Black Dragon King should keep monsters away for a time, but these monsters we've seen are far too unpredictable. I'm making the call to retreat! And—listen carefully—the fact that we came across the black dragon is confidential! Until I give the word, keep tight-lipped about the whole thing! Understood?"

"Yes, sir!"

Zackary turned away from his subordinates and started east. "It's safe to assume the monsters Gideon's unit was fighting have also run away, but we should still check on him."

Soon enough, we crossed paths with Quentin and his unit. "Zackary!" Quentin exclaimed. "I just checked on Gideon's unit—

they're fine. It seems that the monsters fled after seeing the Black Dragon King's sublime form... Oh, just the sight of it alone is enough to strike fear in the hearts of monsters! How divine!"

Zackary paused for what felt like an eternity. Finally, wearily, he spoke. "Great."

A-amazing! You've got to be awful nice not call Quentin out for being a huge weirdo!

"All right!" Zackary bellowed. "Let's withdraw!" Then, suddenly, he slumped his wide shoulders, sighed, and began to grumble. "Planned for a week-long expedition and it didn't even take an hour! An expedition? It was barely a *picnic*!"

It only took about ten minutes to return to the forest entrance.

"All right, break into your units for lunch!" Zackary instructed in his clear, commanding voice. "After lunch, I'll come around and talk to each unit!"

The knights started their preparations. Thinking I should help out too, I began moving to rejoin Zackary's unit when I felt a hand grab my collar. I looked back in surprise to see Zackary himself standing there, wearing a sinister smile.

"With me, Fia. *You* will be eating lunch with Quentin and me."

"Huh?" I blurted. *What's this dark, foreboding aura around him? Is he...mad?* "Th-there's a weirdly menacing aura surrounding you, Captain Zackary! And someone like *me* has no right to eat together with two capt—*hey*, let me go! Just overlook me this one time, please? There's some stuff I need to think about alone..." *Like about how Zavilia's gone, or when Zavilia might be coming back—stuff like that!*

But Zackary just kept on fake-smiling as he dragged me away by the collar. "Oh, really? Why don't you let this older, more experienced captain lend you an ear?"

"H-help! Somebody help!" I made eye contact with a number of knights as they dragged me away, pleading with my eyes, but everyone just waved back with a wry smile. "You're all tacitly supporting this abuse of power, you know!"

He dragged me a distance away before sitting me on the ground—Quentin was already there.

"Speak!" Zackary snapped. "I don't care how long it takes, either! You two better fill me in on every single nitty-gritty little secret you're hiding!" He sat down on the ground beside us and folded his arms. His face was still as stone—yeah, he was dead set on grilling us.

Jeez. Déjà vu, huh? This felt like the beginning of an interrogation—and here was my interrogator, Zackary. Quentin was with me, so we outnumbered him two to one, but...I saw nothing but disaster ahead.

24
Questioned by the Sixth Knight Brigade Captain

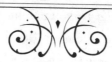

"SPEAK? About what?" Quentin was the first to open his mouth, eyeing Zackary dubiously. Then, as if looking back on a fond memory, his expression changed to one of ecstasy. "Unless—do you want to talk about the Black Dragon King? Of course you do! Ohhh, how *divine*! I still can't fathom how dragons can evolve to reach such levels of heavenly beauty! Surely, you understand?! The Black Dragon King's presence alone makes one want to kneel to it! Its being is absolute perf—"

"Enough!" Zackary interrupted Quentin's creepy, trembling rant. "You obviously don't have a clue what I'm getting at! Fia. Talk!"

Ugh, was he really going to go on about *this* again? "I know what you're trying to say, but you're *definitely* wrong!"

"Oh, really? After everything that happened earlier, you're still expecting me to believe that you're *not* involved with him?!" Zackary narrowed his eyes. The veins of his folded arms bulged.

"Come on! Stop exaggerating!"

"Exaggerating?!" He frowned. "You were talking like you were an old friend of his!"

"Huh?! *Friend?!* I've never even *met* that buff bald instructor of yours!" I exclaimed.

His arms fell to his sides, and he gave me a shocked look. "Wait—what in the *world* are you talking about?!"

I raised my voice, exasperated. "It's that buff bald instructor you can't stop talking about! Look at my hair—and I mean really look at it! Do I look bald to you?! Not even my father Dolph is balding yet! Nobody in my family is balding! Drop it, okay? I'm nothing like him!"

Zackary looked at me blankly for a few moments. Cleared his throat. Pulled himself together a little. "I see. So you're *both* idiots who don't understand the severity of the situation...and *sit up straight*!" he roared.

Quentin and I sat up properly at once, backs straight and hands on our knees.

I gasped. Of course, how had I forgotten something so important?

"What's wrong, Fia?" Zackary asked.

I grabbed his collar, panicking. "C-Captain Zackary! A-am I still losing it?!"

"What?"

"Wh-what you said earlier!" I exclaimed. "Th-the hallucinations and stuff?! Oh! *That* must be how you mistook me for some buff bald guy! Wow, hallucinations are pretty crazy, huh..."

"Okay, stop! I never once said you *looked* like a buff bald guy, and you missed the whole point of me bringing up hallucinations!" He sighed wearily. "Aren't I supposed to be asking the questions? Quentin, you get it, right? You explain."

A frown crossed Quentin's face for a moment, then disappeared. "What Zackary is trying to tell you," he said calmly, "is that he would like to worship you as his goddess after discovering you are the master of the all-powerful and magnificent Black Dragon King."

"Like hell!" Zackary broke in. "What *happened* to you, Quentin?! You used to be one of our best knights! Maybe the Commander was right. Anyone who gets involved with Fia goes *weird...*"

"Objection!" I shouted. "Captain Quentin's been weird as long as I've known him! How is this *my* fault?!"

"Ha ha ha!" Quentin cackled. "It's an honor to be considered special by Miss Fia, just as I've always known you to be special from the start!" Great, more mind-boggling Quentin nonsense...

"See, Captain Zackary?! I just insulted him, and he's taking it as a compliment! It's *him*, not *me*!" Zackary just stared at us silently. "Um. C-Captain Zackary?"

He closed his eyes. "I'm *trying* to bring myself down to both of your levels of thinking. So far, everything you've said sounds like nonsense. To tell the truth, I'm amazed at your capacity for spewing such thoroughly confusing drivel that it's baffling even to *me*."

"Huh?" I blushed, not expecting the sudden compliment. "Um...thanks?"

His eyes suddenly shot open, and he buried his head in his hands. "I was wrong to think I could even *communicate* with you buffoons! And by the way, Fia, that just now? It was sarcasm! I might've sounded like I was complimenting you, but I was actually insulting—*why am I even trying to explain this?! Aaaagh!*"

Quentin put a hand on Zackary's shoulder. "My comrade, you've lived life up until now only believing what you see. But there is so much more to the world! Come, my friend! Accept Miss Fia's greatness into your heart and be set free! Accept the truth as I have, and the world shall be your oyster!"

"Shut up!" Zackary bellowed. "Not a single thing out of your mouth makes a lick of sense! I don't wanna hear another word out of you!"

This is going nowhere fast, I thought as the two continue to argue. Maybe we needed to do something constructive?

"Why don't we stop here for now and get something to eat?"

"What?" Zackary blurted. His mouth flapped open and closed like a beached bass. My words seemed to go in one ear and out the other.

I smiled back at him sweetly. "You two are getting all worked up over nothing because you're hungry...like little children, hee hee! I'll go get lunch! You two wait here."

"Fia, wait!" Zackary yelled something, but I pretended not to hear and left.

Hee hee! I can't believe Captain Zackary is the type to get all grumpy when he's hungry. For a captain, he's so childish! I approached the closest unit, Quentin's, and grabbed three people's worth of lunch.

"Thank you very much!" I said. "Oh, and sorry I couldn't help with preparations and all that." Was it just me, or were the other knights kind of...distant?

"N-n-not at all!" a trembling knight replied. "We owe you a lot, after all...I mean, uh...e-eat as much as you'd like!"

"Y-yeah! F-feel free to get seconds! Just ask!" another knight added, not meeting my eye. "We have tons of leftover food because the expedition was cut short!"

"Oooh, thank you! Everyone's so nice, hee hee!" I said with a smile.

The knights murmured at that—

"No...we should be the ones thanking you..."

"Man...we can't even thank her properly because of Zackary's orders..."

—but they were too quiet, and I didn't really hear them.

I turned around, ready to walk back to the captains, only to come face-to-face with Zackary.

"Hi, Zackary! Too hungry to wait? Did you skip breakfast or something?"

He looked exhausted. "Must be nice," he said with a sigh, "to be so easygoing all the time." He took the lunches from my hands and started walking back.

"Wha—hey, stop! You're a captain! Carrying lunches is a recruit's job!" I said.

Without so much as turning around, he groaned at me. "I still haven't decided whether or not I can treat you like any old recruit. Your calmness belies your age."

"Wait...is this another buff bald guy thing?!"

He slumped his shoulders and shook his head. "Fia...*please*, just drop the whole buff bald guy thing. Let's eat. Your brain clearly lacks nutrients. I'll even give you my portion if you want it, all right?"

Captain Zackary started walking away with large, brisk steps... and stopped when he realized I wasn't following. "Let's go!" he said. "I can't sit down until you do!"

Oh my, Captain Zackary! Well, I suppose waiting for the lady to be seated before seating yourself is common sense for a knight as chivalrous as thee! Could do without the yelling, though.

I ran up to Captain Zackary, did a little hop, and landed on the ground with my legs folded, sitting all comfy. "*Ta-da!* How's that? Impressed?"

"I...take it all back," Zackary groaned. "You're just a kid." He handed me my lunch. I unwrapped it to find one of my favorites inside, white bread! I dug into the bun, tearing off small pieces and stuffing them into my mouth, when I noticed Zackary just staring at me.

"You can eat yours," I said. "I'm not a glutton, you know. I don't *actually* want your lunch. There's a bunch of extra food too, since we prepared a week's worth but finished in a day! I can just go fetch some more if I'm still hungry."

He sighed again and then unwrapped his lunch. With just two bites, he finished his bread.

I watched him, wide-eyed. "Wow, you eat fast!"

"You're easily amused, aren't you?" Another sigh. "I guess my brain lacked nutrients as well. *Fia!*"

Hearing my name said so formally, I straightened my back and responded, "Sir!"

He straightened his back as well and, with his hands on his knees, bowed deeply. "Allow me to express my gratitude."

"Huh?" In my surprise, I accidentally tried to breathe in the piece of bread in my mouth, getting it stuck right in my windpipe. *"Ech, kh, ach!"*

But Zackary, with his head bowed, didn't notice my struggling. "As captain, it should be my responsibility to protect the lives of my knights. And yet the only reason we made it through the day without casualties is thanks to you, Fia. So please, allow me to express my gratitude as a captain."

"N—*koff, koff*—not—*koff*—at all, Captain Zackary! I didn't do a thing. Today is all thanks to Zav—thanks to the black dragon and all the other knights. So, uh...please raise your head!" I said, stumbling to find the words needed to make him stop after the bread lodged in my throat finally went down.

Just when I thought he'd never look up, he raised his head—and the look on his face was deadly serious. "Fia, you used some hidden power of yours to protect everyone, didn't you."

"Hwah?!" I yelped out of sheer surprise. "Wh-wh-wh-wh-wh-wh-what? Wh-who, me?!"

Quentin, sitting next to me, was also surprised. "What?! Miss Fia, you were trying to *hide* your power? I thought you were boldly displaying your capability without care, but perhaps that was just my poor, feeble misunderstanding! So, Miss Fia, which of your powers are you trying to hide?" He tried to whisper the next part, though Zackary was completely in earshot. "Might I... somehow be of some assistance?"

At my wits' end, I buried my face in my hands and just screamed. "Aaaaaaaaaarrrrrgh!" *How much does Captain Zackary know?! And is Captain Quentin an obnoxious friend or an obnoxious foe?!*

My head still buried in my hands, my mind racing, Zackary continued. "You knew how to fight the Green Nightmare. You knew the Flower-Horned Deer's unique traits. You knew the numbers and types of monsters the other units were fighting even though you couldn't see them. Somehow, you *controlled* the other knights' familiars. In the end, you even commanded the black dragon. Every one of these things is—or should be—impossible."

I said nothing.

"For whatever reason, you're hiding your power...and yet you risked exposure to help us today. For that reason, I've decided that I'll respect whatever you're doing. I won't get in your way," he said with a tone of finality.

I peeked through my hands. "Captain Zackary?" I felt so silly, peering through my fingers at him.

As for him, he looked as serious as could be. "Above all things, I am a knight. I have sworn by the Ten Knight Commandments. To go against your wishes—the wishes of my savior—would break those Commandments and abandon my pride as a knight.

I swear on my position as captain of the Sixth Knight Brigade, I will keep your secret, Fia. I shall do whatever I can to protect you."

"Captain Zackary..."

"I mean it. I plan to keep this promise until the day I die. Let me apologize too, for being so roundabout about these things. I should've simply told you outright." He paused for a moment, his expression softening a bit. "You don't need to tell me everything. Only share what you're comfortable sharing."

He said nothing more. He merely crossed his arms and waited for my reply.

Overcome with emotion, I couldn't muster a voice. *Captain Zackary...you really are a man among men.*

I stared back at Zackary in silence. What could I even say after that display of manliness?

The first to speak was not me but Quentin. "Zackary, I have reason to believe that those feats you listed were all made possible by the great Black Dragon King's power."

Zackary furrowed his brows. "Oh? You think so?"

Quentin nodded deeply. "Yes. I'm sure you've realized by now, but the Blue Dove that often rode on Fia's shoulder was actually the Black Dragon King in disguise. Records show that the Black Dragon King has been around for at least a thousand years, meaning he would have at least a thousand years' worth of knowledge and power. Naturally, he would know the traits of monsters, could sense monsters from a distance, could even control the other knights' familiars..."

"Is that true, Fia?" Zackary asked.

"Um...hmm. I'm sure that Zav—that the black dragon—probably knows monsters well, and I *did* get the information about what each unit was fighting from him. But controlling other familiars? I...*guess* he can let out a low wail to make other monsters obey."

W-wait! Doesn't that mean Zavilia's been helping with, like, everything? W-well, those things aren't a saint's job anyway! Y-yeah... it's normal to get a little help...isn't it?

Feeling pathetic all of a sudden, I looked up at Zackary. He stared at me silently for some time before nodding his head understandingly. "All right. If that's the answer you want to give, then that's the answer I'll accept."

Huh? Well, that's a loaded sentence. I mean, it's the truth, you know? Just...with all the saint parts left out.

The real reason I knew so much about monsters was because I'd fought so many in my previous life, and the real reason I could control other knights' familiars was because they were attracted to the smell of my blood...but I couldn't just say any of that. Or could I? Was now the time to finally come clean to somebody?

The moment the thought crossed my mind, I began to tremble. My heart pounded. Sweat ran down my face and back. Even breathing grew difficult... My breaths came short and shallow.

"Fia?" Zackary asked worriedly.

I have to calm down, I thought, but my body was practically pulling me to the ground. Dragging me into a collapse.

I stayed like that, breathing shallowly, gasping.

I can't...

Memories from my past life came rushing back.

He's too strong...

Zackary and Quentin were both strong. Zavilia was *incredibly* strong. Even Saviz and Cyril were powerful. But they paled in comparison to the Demon Lord's right-hand man...

If it got out that I was a saint, he would kill me. I just *knew* he would kill me. Even if Zackary and Quentin and Zavilia and Saviz and Cyril all tried to protect me, it'd end with their meaningless deaths.

I lay on the ground. It hurt to breathe. Short, shallow breaths. It hurt so much that I couldn't stop tears from welling in my eyes.

It hurts...

But the thought of them dying because of me hurt even more. I wanted to return Zackary's kindness with the truth, but I couldn't...not when it might get everyone killed... I just *knew* they couldn't beat that demon, not even if they fought a hundred times.

It wasn't that I thought Zackary couldn't keep my secret, but I couldn't let him bear that risk. He promised he wouldn't tell anyone, even swore on his position as captain...and that was why it hurt so much that I couldn't tell him. For all the goodwill he showed me, I couldn't return it at all...

I did nothing to stop the tears from streaming down. I took heaving gasps for air.

"Fia..."

I glanced up—I couldn't move my head, but I could move my eyes—at the sound of his voice. He didn't say anything further. Instead, he delicately picked me up in his arms. My head was pressed against his heart. My breathing was still pained and shallow, and my consciousness started to grow faint.

"Fia, can you hear my heartbeat?" His voice was so much gentler than usual.

Focusing on my ears, I could hear the slow, steady sound of Zackary's powerful heartbeat. Robbed of words, I could only nod.

"Good. Try to match your heartbeat with mine. Breathe in slowly, then breathe out still more slowly...yes, just like that." His big, warm hands gently brushed up and down my back. My tears stained his uniform, but he didn't seem to mind—he kept talking to me gently, helping me breathe. Slowly, my breathing normalized, and my trembling and sweating died down. Even so, I stayed in his arms for a while, eyes shut, letting my turbulent mind calm.

I felt bad, but the truth was simple—I couldn't tell Zackary. No matter how many times this situation played out, I'd end up making the same choice. In my past life, the knights would always insist that I was far more important than they were. To them, knights were the shield of the Great Saint, but never vice versa.

I'd always rejected that idea. Knight or saint, we were all equal. Just as knights would be the shield of the saints, I swore to be the shield of the knights. I would protect them as they had protected me. That's why I couldn't tell Zackary the truth now... I had to protect him from that truth.

Having finally made up my mind, I took a deep sigh.

Noticing I'd calmed down, Zackary took his hand off my back. "I'm sorry, Fia. I shouldn't have pushed you to answer. Let's leave things at this for now. Here." He offered his waterskin. "Do you think you could drink some water?"

I'd only intended to quench my thirst a little, but once I tasted the water, I couldn't stop gulping it down until it was all gone. Feeling invigorated, I put a hand on Zackary's chest and smiled up at him. "Thank you, Captain Zackary. I'm feeling better now."

"You certainly bounce back quickly," he said with a relieved smile, patting my back like he was comforting a small child.

"Thank you for promising to keep my secret, Captain Zackary, but...I'm sorry. I don't think I can tell you any more than I already have," I said.

He stared at me as though to ascertain whether this was truly my own decision. I stared back resolutely to show him that it was. He soon after gave a small, understanding nod.

"All right," he whispered, looking into my eyes somberly. "Just remember, we are in your debt. You don't need to tell us what you aren't ready to. However, if you ever change your mind, just call for me. I'll come running. That's the least I can do to show my gratitude." He lifted me off his lap, helping me stand. "Now, then—you're tired. Go ahead and head back to the castle first. I have to stay here and explain what I can, but I'll send a few knights with you."

I wondered why I didn't need to stay and hear like everyone else, but he was right that I was exhausted and probably would just get in the way right now. If a captain deemed me unfit and ordered me to return, I couldn't object. Still, I felt uncomfortable making a few knights escort me back.

"Um, I don't want to bother anyone. Why don't I just head back to the castle alone?"

He paused for a moment. "It's fine," he said. "They have business at the castle."

Captain Zackary was lying. *He's really worried about me...but I'm fine now! What's he afraid of happening on the way back? It's not like I'm going to fall off my horse or something...* Still, it'd be rude to reject his kindness. I rolled with it.

I was readying my horse for return, fastening on my bag, when Zackary came up. "Fia," he said seriously, "I have to report what happened today to Commander Saviz. But I swear to you that I won't bring you any trouble."

His words made me realize just how little I'd explained to him. Submitting a report to the Commander with what little information I'd given him wouldn't be easy...and yet he was still trying to reassure me that everything would be okay.

I couldn't help but sigh. *You really are a man among men, Zackary...*

Zackary, Captain of the Sixth Knight Brigade

MY NAME is Zackary Townsend, captain of the Sixth Knight Brigade.

The first time I saw Fia was at the welcome ceremony. The ceremony went as it did every year—until the sudden announcement that Commander Saviz would be participating in the exhibition match. Surely, the announcer was joking or crazy, but the pale look on the announcer's face made me realize that they were quite serious. *Ah. The Commander must have put them up to this.*

The Commander seemed like the serious type, but I knew he actually had a playful side. Still, I couldn't help but wonder if it was just playfulness or something more sadistic when a young girl stepped forward to be his opponent—to take on Saviz himself. What meaning could there be in a match against her? She didn't look like she could withstand a blow, much less *stand*, with how much she was shaking. She walked nervously, the same foot and arm swinging forward as she moved. It would've gotten a laugh from me if it were two of my subordinates fighting, but against the Commander? I only felt pity.

That was when Ardio, a well-known knight with the moniker "The Knight of Ice," and his younger brother Leon ran up to the young girl and said something.

Ah...she must be Dolph's daughter, then. I recalled Dolph, the vice-captain of the Fourteenth Knight Brigade, having three kids in the Knight Brigades. This girl must've been the fourth. *She's a bit small for Dolph's kid, though. Tough luck—she probably wasn't blessed with a good physique.*

Perhaps she had some skill with the sword, being born to a knight family, but she surely wasn't going to last one blow against the Commander—not with a body like that. At least she'd have a happy memory to look back on later; being the Commander's opponent itself was a great honor.

The girl then gave her name, Fia Ruud, and dashed forward toward the Commander.

Hm...it's impressive enough she didn't freeze up, I thought, genuinely surprised, when she suddenly sped up five meters before the Commander, drew her sword at an abnormal speed, and swung.

A sharp *twang* resounded as I watched the Commander brace his entire body to block.

How heavy is that sword? I thought, noticing the sound her blade made.

I watched in surprise as Fia swung again and again at the Commander, the intervals shortening with each swing. But what really caught my attention was how she focused on striking the same side.

What is she aiming for? I wondered as I watched the fight unblinking—only for it to abruptly end with her sword being knocked away.

The knights erupted in cheers...but my eyes were drawn to the Commander, who bit his lip in frustration.

She managed to make *him*, of all people, feel like he had lost.

He soon after declared the match invalid. It came to light that her weapon was a magic sword with incredible enhancements, but even more problematic was the reason that she kept attacking the same side of the Commander. Pressed for answers, she admitted that she'd discovered an old leg injury by analyzing his movements.

She's a recruit? I thought, shaking my head in disbelief. I took a good, hard look at her. It hadn't been long since the Commander had entered the ceremony grounds, but in that short span of time, she'd uncovered his old combat wound. It was incredible, too, that she hadn't frozen up before him—even with her magic sword, not many could fight the Commander without cowering.

It was unimaginable. But even more unthinkable was her reasoning for taking advantage of the Commander's weakness, boldly claiming it was her "chivalry as a knight" with a suspiciously straight face—an obvious lie.

This girl's got guts of steel to lie to the Commander...

That day, the Commander declared that he would remember Fia Ruud's name. I did the same.

I next met Fia at a feast. My brigade had returned from a successful expedition with monster meat in tow, so we decided to celebrate with an informal gathering where we ate meat and drank—we called it a "meat festival."

But before the feast began, Cyril called for me. Two recruits from his brigade had been tagging along with mine for training—had there been a problem with them? I had been busy and hadn't had time to hear how the expedition went directly from my subordinates. When a knight from the First Knight Brigade came to pick me up at the canteen, I followed him without knowing what was going on.

I was led to a room. There stood some of my knights who had embarked on today's expedition standing across from Cyril, who wore an unnerving smile, and the Commander, whose expression was unreadable.

Something displeasing had occurred—I knew that at once. I watched my knights' faces as I stepped before Cyril and the Commander.

Cyril smiled stiffly. "Thank you for coming, Zackary. I was just commending these knights for their wonderful performance on today's expedition."

I glanced at Cyril's stiff smile, then looked back to my knights. *That's a lie. What the hell did you guys do to piss Cyril off this badly?*

Before I could ask, two more knights entered the room. One of them was Fia.

Huh. So she was one of the recruits assigned to today's expedition.

Cyril made all the knights, including Fia, sit down in chairs. I moved to a position where I could stare down on everyone. The Commander stayed behind me, silently watching. His presence made me sure that whatever had happened was serious. I folded my arms and watched silently as well.

Cyril explained what had happened: a monster from the deep forest had appeared, and it was defeated without casualty, thanks to the splendid performance of the knights. The problem, though, was that the one who took command during the encounter wasn't one of the experienced knights of the Sixth Knight Brigade.

It was Fia, a recruit from his brigade.

What in the world...?

Cyril's voice was as cold as ice and his smile as frigid as a demon's as he pressed the knights for answers. He was livid. In an attempt to calm my own rage, I closed my eyes. Sighed. Opened my eyes and glared at my knights.

What the hell were you all thinking?!

But my knights were smart enough to know that speaking would only make things worse, and so Cyril singled out Fia. The girl promptly spilled the beans, but her words only confused me. She claimed to have taken command and defeated a monster with knowledge from a reference book and experiences she'd had in *dreams*!

That's nonsense! How could anyone lead so calmly while analyzing a monster they'd never seen, and accompanied by so few knights? It's impossible. If it were that easy, we'd have rid the forest of monsters ages ago.

I looked on with exasperation as she continued, explaining how she determined the intervals between the monster's attack and calculated the monster's health. I couldn't help but smile wryly when she talked about that last part—why, such a method would require one to fight the same monster hundreds of times, if not thousands!

Just who *was* this recruit? This *abnormality* mixed in with the knights. But the part that shocked me most was what followed—Fia fought back against Cyril.

Everyone had gone pale in the face of Cyril's icy smile, gloomily staring down at their feet. Fia alone dared to look Cyril in the eye and declare that her hands were meant to be holding delicious meat and drink this very moment.

This girl's got guts. She'd talked back to the highest-ranking captain, and in front of the Commander at that. Needless to say, my interest in her was piqued...but I'm ashamed of what happened later that night. I don't remember much, but what I do remember is rather embarrassing to my knightly pride.

I remember Fia's bulging, toddler-like chubby belly, I remember her lamenting about training every day but not gaining any muscle, and I remember not knowing what to say to all of her loaded questions. She was right—I had no right to complain about my four-pack when there were those less fortunate than me in this world, like Fia. Since then, I haven't complained once about my abdominals. I do, however, wish I could completely wipe the sight of Fia's belly from my mind—because that's the chivalrous thing to do, of course.

The third time I met Fia, she was with Quentin. She greeted me formally, as though talking to a stranger—probably because she wanted to forget how she'd so embarrassingly displayed her belly. I did too.

I'd heard from Cyril that Quentin was mentally unwell after his long expedition, but I hadn't expected his state to be so dire. Usually well groomed, Quentin was *wet* for some reason when he appeared, an early indication that something was off. Concerned, I asked him what had happened, only for him to plainly state that *Miss* Fia had spat water onto him!

You haven't wiped yourself off, and now you're calling her Miss *Fia?!*

I watched, confused, as Fia reprimanded Quentin for his word choice. The latter apologized profusely. The sight was so revolting that a shiver ran down my back.

What the hell...? Did Quentin awaken to some strange fetish? He used to be a lone wolf kind of guy who performed his duties as a captain properly. We hadn't talked much, but he always kept things brief, giving just the right warning and advice. He'd been a model knight. What could've changed him so much in the half-year I hadn't seen him? I hoped Cyril was right, that this was just stress from his long expedition, that he would be back to normal eventually...

When the Commander entered the room, I breathed a sigh of relief—finally, things would get back to normal. But then *Cyril*, of all people, began to argue with Quentin over Fia!

What *was* this? Was there some infectious disease driving everyone bonkers? Cyril was a duke! He was the captain of the First Knight Brigade! He *should* be as logical as they came, easily suppressing his true emotions and manipulating others. And now he was losing it too?

In an attempt to calm things down, I offered to let her stand behind me. In response, Cyril and Quentin turned their necks lightning-fast and glared at me.

These two are sick in the head, I thought, but it turned out that the sickest one there was Fia. Ignoring the three of us, she walked over and chose Clarissa, the Fifth Knight Brigade captain.

Just trying to understand what was going on in Fia's brain was giving me a headache. She looked positively *happy* standing behind Clarissa.

What an easygoing girl. I bet she's the sort who always finds a way to be happy, even if it's at everyone else's expense. Ah, poor Cyril!

Sometime later, I spotted Quentin and his slightly irksome vice-captain Gideon fawning over Fia. Gideon was on his knee *begging* for some reason. Odd, that. He'd always been the cynical sort, not the type to kneel down to someone half his height.

Eerie. Is that really Gideon, or am I mistaking him for some-one else? I thought, and I decided to call out to him. From his response, I had no choice but to believe it was him.

Anyone who dealt with Fia seemed to become stranger in one way or another. It worried me, but the black dragon hunt was coming up, so I decided to put it aside. Looking back on it, I think I was right. It would have been a waste of time to worry about her. You see, what I saw that day blew all of those worries out the window.

On that day, every single action Fia took defied logic. The advice she gave for fighting the Green Nightmare and Flower-Horned Deer was perfect. Even if, as Quentin and Fia later insisted, the black dragon had told her what to say...well, she was far too calm, and her advice was far too precise for the intensity of the situation.

Then there was her command of the familiars. Quentin and Fia pinned it on the black dragon once again, but I saw the way the familiars moved. They were *definitely* looking at Fia and not the black dragon. I doubted that Quentin, an expert on familiars, would make such a mistake. Perhaps he was trying to mislead me for some reason? I would have to question him later.

There was also the problem of how the blue dragons beelined straight for Fia. Back when Cyril was questioning her, we learned that she took command because the unit's leader was knocked unconscious by the Flower-Horned Deer. The Flower-Horned Deer, being a B-rank monster, was smart enough to determine who was in command at a glance and take them out to cause confusion. Which begged the question—why didn't the S-rank blue dragons target Quentin or me? The only possibility was that Fia was somehow a more important target.

But why? For whatever reason, the blue dragons had immediately seen something within her that I could not, as had the black dragon.

I never could've imagined that the ancient and legendary black dragon, one of the continent's Three Great Beasts, would be Fia's familiar. However she'd managed to make a pact with such a powerful being, it was clear as day that he was loyal to her. He protected her, fought for her, even cut off his own horn for her. That last act of cutting off his own horn in particular struck me as something that went beyond a normal master-familiar relationship. It was like he was marking Fia so nobody would mess with her. Just what had she done to gain the black dragon's favor?

A deep sigh escaped my lips as I contemplated the never-ending pile of problems. Frustration, irritation, and a plethora of other emotions swelled inside me...but the strongest of those emotions was gratitude toward Fia.

She was hiding something, something that would likely explain the web of mysteries surrounding her...but even so, I knew in my heart that she was a good soul.

Despite how much her secret clearly meant to her, she'd willingly jeopardized it to save everyone. Because of that, not a single life was lost. I've had brushes with death countless times. A mission with no casualties can be a miracle.

But still, I thought after reflecting on how much I owed her, *she's doing a dreadful job of hiding her secret. It's a wonder nobody's figured it out.*

Fia lacked resolve. Her secret was clearly important to her, so why risk it being revealed to save the lives of a few knights? If she wasn't willing to make that sacrifice, why hide it at all? It felt like only a matter of time before her secret would be forced into the light...

Whatever secrets lay behind the curtain, the simplest answers often proved correct. Whatever her secrets, whatever was behind the cloud of mysteries surrounding her, it was likely something very simple—something insignificant to anyone but her.

Most secrets prove insignificant in the light of day.

I wanted to tell her this, to encourage her to confide in me, but I couldn't. Not after witnessing her panic attack. She was fighting her own battle, an internal conflict over whether or not to reveal her secret...and she'd made her choice.

She didn't trust me.

At that moment, I wanted to kick myself for how useless I was. I couldn't do a thing for her as she lay on the ground, drenched in sweat, struggling to breathe. Even when she could finally speak, it was only to say she couldn't tell me her secret. I remember her eyes then, so fierce and determined.

The ferocity in those eyes...just what was she trying to protect?

Based on her actions so far, she was probably trying to protect others. As pathetic as it made me feel, she was probably trying to protect me as well.

Whatever her secret was, she kept it for our sake...and it tore me up inside that I couldn't repay her for it, that I couldn't be someone she could confide in.

So, in the end, Fia is protecting me. I let out a deep, full-body sigh and flexed my folded arms. *The other captains would probably have a good laugh if they knew.*

I had to become stronger.

Strong enough to become someone Fia could confide in.

Strong enough to be her shield the next time we faced a powerful monster.

How could I call myself a captain otherwise?

I sighed, trying to let out some of the frustration at my useless self, hoping to refresh my mind. The knights were at lunch with their units.

What was the best way to handle this situation?

Each of the three units had different understandings of what went down today. I wasn't sure whether it'd be better to share information with everyone to prepare for whatever incident Fia caused next or to try to mitigate potential risk by only telling a few people.

Still conflicted, I glanced at Quentin by my side. I currently lacked the information needed to make a proper judgment, but perhaps Quentin could help with that?

"Quentin, come with me for a bit. There's some things I need to ask you." We moved away from the other knights, just past the trees. Once there, I moved my face close to his—a habit of mine when interrogating others.

"When I asked you how likely we were to find the black dragon this morning," I said, "you stated that it was one hundred percent. You've known Fia's familiar was the black dragon for some time now, haven't you?"

"Of course," Quentin said nonchalantly.

How infuriating! "'Of course' my ass! Why'd you keep quiet about something so important?!"

"Miss Fia and her familiar, the Black Dragon King himself, didn't explicitly state his identity. What right did I have to tell you?"

"Don't give me that! This is a *black dragon* we're talking about! An expert like you, of all people, should know how big a deal it is for someone to make the black dragon their familiar! Why didn't you report it?!"

"Precisely because I'm an expert. As I'm sure you're aware, the width of a master's proof of pact is proportionate to the time it took to make the familiar submit to a pact." Quentin rolled up his sleeves. I could see his proof of pact—a scaly line coiling around like a snake, stretching from his wrist upward onto his upper arm.

"This is from the time I made a griffon, an A-rank, my familiar. It took a long time to make it submit, and so it stretches to my shoulder. Because the griffon resisted, the line is broken in many places. This is normal. But what Fia has is completely different. Her proof of pact is only one millimeter. It has no breaks whatsoever, even though the Black Dragon King is an SS-rank monster. It's perfect! She somehow got the strongest monster to swear absolute obedience to her in no time at all."

"I...see," I murmured, nodding.

Quentin shook his head. "No, Zackary, you *don't* see. A familiar with absolute obedience can read their master's emotions, meaning the familiar can make their own judgments and act freely on their master's behalf without orders! Now, what do you think would happen if I were to reveal that Miss Fia's familiar was the Black Dragon King without her explicit approval? The Black Dragon King himself would kill me and anybody who heard on the spot!" He paused. "At least, that's what I think."

I said nothing. A shiver ran down my spine.

Observing my silence, Quentin continued. "Miss Fia told me the circumstances leading up to her making a pact with the Black Dragon King. He had reverted to infancy due to sustaining fatal wounds when Fia fed him a healing potion...but I have doubts about her story. It shouldn't be possible for an external factor to heal wounds that the Black Dragon King's natural regeneration couldn't already heal."

Quentin pushed his hair back and stared up at the empty sky, as if he was living the conversation again. "But it must be true," he said. "I see no reason that Miss Fia would need to lie. I suspect that she omitted something important, something needed to grasp the full picture, but I absolutely won't ask what. If the Black Dragon King deemed me a nuisance, I'd be killed."

"You're kidding..." I muttered. It was one shock after another.

"Well...the important thing to remember is that it doesn't actually matter how Fia herself feels. If the Black Dragon King believes you're causing her problems, then you're dragon food. Or worse."

"She's picked up an absolute monster..." I whispered. A black dragon wasn't something you should carelessly make a pact with, even if it was injured. Just what was she thinking?

But Quentin sounded downright spirited. "Not just any monster, but the legendary, ancient black dragon! He can read Miss Fia's emotions even when separated, so you'd better not do anything foolish!"

"Ah." I let out a long sigh. "Wonderful." It felt like my back was against the wall.

Quentin looked at me with pity for a moment before he suddenly seemed to realize something. "You should be more careful interacting with Miss Fia. Just earlier, she seemed to have a sudden breakdown because you kept pelting her with questions. If she felt even the slightest bit of ill will toward you, the Black Dragon King would have torn a hole in the sky, appeared, and killed you."

"Hey, wait—is that why you took off? I thought you'd left out of consideration for Fia!"

"You misunderstand! I was ensuring at least one of us would survive to make a report."

"That's...acceptable. But I still want to punch you for some reason..."

"Because you're petty."

"Hah, right. Now shut it before I punch you for real." I took a deep breath and bit back the urge to clock Quentin, then I folded my arms and leaned against a nearby tree.

"Anyway," said Quentin, straight-faced as ever, "we need to be careful. If, for example, we report what happened today to the

Commander and the Black Dragon King deems it a problem for Fia, he might target him. But I doubt that will happen, seeing as the Black Dragon King decided to give us his own horn."

"The horn? What has that got to do with anything?"

"We have the Black Dragon King's approval. The horn is a valuable rare material that can be used to create a sword. The thing is, however, it is nearly impossible to break off. The only way to get it is if the Black Dragon King granted it to us on his own accord. Anyone who saw the horn will understand this, so I can only assume the Black Dragon King is permitting us to tell our allies about him. I'm thinking it should also be okay if we tell others that Fia's familiar is the Black Dragon King...although not *too* many."

"How certain are you?"

"At best, thirty percent."

"You had so much confidence when you predicted the black dragon's appearance. Where did *that* go?"

"The Commander's life—the lives of *many* knights—are hanging in the balance. I can't give in to wishful thinking."

"Hmph. So you're back to normal once Fia's gone, huh?" I raised an eyebrow. He was surprisingly sensible again.

"The Black Dragon King clearly treasures Miss Fia. It should be okay to tell others as long as it ends up benefitting her."

"She's already got the black dragon backing her. What can we do that would even count as benefiting her at this point?" I rubbed my neck with my hand. "And Fia herself poses a problem. As far as I can gather, she's just as dangerous as the black dragon. Letting her run loose might bite us in the ass one day..."

"It won't," he said. "Miss Fia is too kind."

"Hm?" I furrowed my brow.

"Human emotions are unpredictable," said Quentin. "Another's actions or words can sometimes incite sudden rage or murderous impulses within us. Of course, we don't act on these feelings, and they fade shortly afterward. But monsters aren't like that. No, they simply kill what's bothering them on the spot."

"Sure. They're just beasts after all." Where was he going with this?

"That being the case, it's strange the Black Dragon King hasn't killed anyone yet. It should take some time for the Black Dragon King to understand that Miss Fia's feelings toward others change with time, yet not a single person has died. I think she's simply too kindhearted to bear deep resentment toward others. Even when my vice-captain Gideon treated her poorly, the most the Black Dragon King did was retaliate with some childish harassment. She probably didn't feel anything more than annoyance at Gideon."

"I see. You know, I can't see Fia as the grudge-holding type either."

"A person's nature doesn't change easily. We can assume that she will stay as she is and will not pose a threat to us. Besides, if we locked people up for being powerful, that would include both of us as well, along with the Commander and Cyril. If you really felt like it, you could kill around a hundred knights before they stopped you, no?"

"I...could," I said.

"And yet I don't think you're dangerous at all."

"Gee, thanks." His words convinced me, but her family background left some questions.

"Fia's the youngest daughter in her family, right?" I mused. "Maybe she grew up sheltered, showered in love, and never learned how to distrust or hate others." It was the first thing I'd thought of.

"It's likely. Miss Fia is unbelievably naive. She was free to do as she wished, loved by everyone in her territory."

I stood up from the tree I was slumping against, and the two of us returned to the main group. As I walked back, I reaffirmed to myself my decision: we would keep today's events under wraps.

I visited each unit and ordered them to not share any information with knights outside of their unit. Then I visited the commander with Quentin and Gideon. I kept the report superficial, saying that we met the black dragon, but its size was too great to attempt making a pact with, so we threw a stone from Blackpeak Mountain and succeeded in getting it to return to its nest. I finished by saying that I'd add to my report when the time was right. The Commander seemed to pick up somewhat on my intent and excused us, commending us for our efforts.

Just blindly reporting everything to the Commander would be foolish. I had a duty to keep him safe, even if it meant hiding things from him. That said, I had no qualms about endangering that bloodthirsty captain Cyril. The same with Desmond, whose position as commandant of the Military Police required him to know everything. If the black dragon didn't appear for some time after we told those two everything, we could safely assume that we were permitted to tell others. Then, and only then, would we tell the commander.

Together with Quentin and Gideon, I headed to the conference room where Cyril and Desmond waited.

A Tale of the
Secret
Saint

A Small Meeting Among Captains

"I THOUGHT THE EXPEDITION was going to last a week. What happened?"

No sooner had Zackary, Quentin, and Gideon opened the door to the conference room than they heard Cyril speak from within. Zackary raised an eyebrow—surprisingly, the usually prim and proper Cyril wasn't waiting for them to sit before asking questions. It was surprising enough that Cyril and Desmond had somehow reached the room before them—after all, they'd been called by the three of them mere moments ago—but more pressing was how on edge they were, glaring at the three as they entered the room.

Zackary briskly moved to a chair, glancing at the object atop the round table as he sat. Confirming everyone was seated, he calmly began, "First thing's first. The expedition was a success, and no casualties were incurred."

"What?!" Desmond was surprised. "You got the Black King to return in just half a day? Impossible!"

From the next seat over, Cyril looked at Zackary with a skeptical gaze. "You only left this morning. Accounting for the time it'd take to get to Starfall Forest and back, you should've hardly had time to do anything more than assemble into units at the entrance. I can't see you finishing your mission so quickly."

Zackary nodded soberly. "I understand your doubts, and I'd probably think the same thing if I were in your shoes. It'd be faster to start off by discussing why I called you two here, if that's all right."

Cyril and Desmond nodded. Zackary continued. "Early on into the expedition, we came across some top-secret information. The information in question is too dangerous, so we've chosen to reveal only a fraction of it to the Commander. I've also issued a gag order to the knights involved."

Zackary's expression clouded. "The decision to not tell the Commander was mine," he added, "as was the decision to call you two here. Cyril...as captain of the most prestigious brigade, you have a responsibility to oversee all that happens within it. Desmond, as commandant of the Military Police, you have a responsibility to know of dangerous events within the brigades. But hearing this information will pose a risk to your lives. Are you okay with that?"

Cyril was unfazed. "Need you ask? My life was the Kingdom's the moment I became a knight. Risking my life is to be expected."

Desmond was just as unmoved. "Same as him, thank you very much. I wouldn't have become a captain in the first place if I wasn't willing to risk my life in the line of duty."

Zackary was surprised by their clear, resolute answers. "I see.

I didn't mean to insult you two. The position of captain doesn't necessarily entail this sort of risk, though, and I doubt most people would be as unperturbed as you two after hearing this. You're both knights I'm proud to serve with."

He whispered the last bit, more so to himself, and then looked to Gideon. "Gideon," said Zackary, "you're free to leave if you wish. Hearing this information will endanger your life. The information in question is something you missed due to being in a separate unit. It concerns a familiar, so—you being the vice-captain of the Fourth Monster Tamer Knight Brigade—it'd be better for us if you knew in case something happens to Quentin. But the choice is yours to make."

Gideon didn't hesitate. "I-I'll stay! I'm a proud knight of the Fourth Monster Tamer Knight Brigade! Let me do what I can to help!"

Zackary gave a light nod, the corner of his lips turning upward slightly. "You're marvelous, each and every one of you." He folded his arms and met everyone's eyes. "I'll start, then. To reiterate, we did in fact succeed in moving the Black King out of Starfall Forest. As for *how* we did so in a mere half day...that's where things get complicated..." Zackary turned to Cyril. "Were you aware that Fia has a familiar?" he asked casually.

"An odd question," said Cyril, "but yes. She showed it to me. It was a bluebird-type monster called a Blue Dove, if I remember correctly. It seemed rather fond of Fia, and I recall that her proof of pact was strangely thin." He gave Zackary a curious look that seemed to say, *What of it?*

Straight-faced, Zackary looked Cyril in the eyes. "Fia's familiar...is the black dragon."

Cyril blinked. "Huh?"

Desmond furrowed his brow. "Now's really not the time for jokes," he cut in, "especially ones in such bad taste."

The two were impatient, as if waiting for Zackary to hurry up and make his big reveal. Desmond was particularly irritated—he began to crack his knuckles.

Quentin spoke for the first time. "It's the truth, Desmond. The Black Dragon King is Fia's familiar."

"You too, Quentin?" Desmond snarled. "Give me a break! Even I know you can't make a monster your familiar without beating it in a contest of strength! What's next? Fia's some master swordsman who can fight head-to-head with the black dragon?!" He seemed offended, as if Zackary were mocking him. Cyril and Gideon wore doubtful looks as well.

"Being stronger than the monster *is* important," said Zackary patiently, "but there are also cases where the master and monster are naturally compatible. Perhaps something about Fia interested the black dragon?"

"Hmm...hypothetically speaking, if the black dragon was bored from living a thousand years, Fia could be the entertainment it needs," said Cyril thoughtfully. "There certainly is never a dull moment with her." Still, he didn't sound convinced.

"Get real!" Desmond scoffed. "The black dragon spent years holed up in its cave. Why would it get tired of the quiet life now?"

Seeing that words wouldn't convince them, Zackary reached out to an item covered by a sheet that sat atop the round table—it was as long as an adult man lying on his side. He pulled the cloth off to reveal a perplexing item, its purpose a mystery at a glance. The item wasn't just long but also oddly conical. Its color was a mystery, shifting from white to black to silver depending on the angle from which it was viewed.

"Is this...a horn?" Cyril gasped, plainly bewildered. "But I've never heard of a creature with horns this large and beautiful..."

Desmond reached out and touched it. "Incredible... This thing absorbs all the magic I emit without any waste. I've never *seen* a magic-absorbing item with this sheer efficiency. What *is* this?"

"It's the horn of the Black Dragon King. He gave it to Zackary and—of course—to *me* as payment for promising to protect Fia," said Quentin.

At once, Cyril, Desmond, and Gideon went silent—each wore a different expression on his face as all three tried to process what they'd just heard. The idea of the black dragon being Fia's familiar was unbelievable, yet it perfectly explained this impossible horn before them.

"I understand that you three won't believe us right away," said Zackary. "Even I still think I'll wake up and discover this was all a dream...but it isn't. Fia's familiar is the black dragon. For now, put aside your preconceptions and believe. I mean, do you truly think I would tell a joke in such bad taste?"

"You certainly haven't before," said Cyril. He looked unconvinced. "But it's still too far-fetched."

Zackary sighed. "Your thinking is understandable, Cyril. When it comes to strength, Fia is far below your average knight. But that's precisely why I believe that she got the black dragon's attention with something other than raw strength."

"According to her," Quentin cut in, "she came across the Black Dragon King by chance when it was gravely injured and had reverted to infancy. She claims to have given it a healing potion, but I'm doubtful that any such potion could do something for the Black Dragon King—it already has the highest natural recovery rate of any monster, after all. In the end, we're not sure how she saved it, but she claims that this is how she formed a pact."

Cyril scrunched his eyes, contemplating. "I don't think you two would go this far for a joke, which leaves us with two possibilities: The first, that the black dragon is genuinely Fia's familiar, and the second, that you two are either delusional or have grossly misunderstood the situation."

"Hmph. Could you possibly hedge your bets any more than that?" Zackary grumbled. "Well...close enough." With that, he slammed his hands against the table. "All right, let's go drink! We got some quality meat from the expedition, so tonight's gonna be a feast. Let's get a few stiff ones somewhere until it's time."

Cyril gave him a look. "What's with you all of a sudden, Zackary? We're not finished here! In fact, we haven't accomplished a single thing yet."

"Yeaaah, well..." Zackary shrugged. "We're straight up out of concrete evidence we can show you guys, so I don't see any use in talking on and on. I mean, you three clearly aren't going to come around. Might as well finish this over drinks." He stood up. "Who knows? Maybe the change of pace will help you see things in a different light."

Cyril laughed. "Oh, I get it now! You really are the same as always, eh? No, there's no delusion or misunderstanding on your part." His expression turned serious once again—Zackary and Quentin exchanged a glance. "So...the black dragon really is Fia's familiar?"

"Yeah..." Zackary replied. "There's gonna be some blue dragon meat at tonight's feast. If you stop by the kitchen, you'll see it was killed not by a blade but the fangs of a beast—by the black dragon's fangs, in fact. It's not uncommon for monsters to fight, sure, but we saw the black dragon move to protect the knights from the blue dragons...completely under Fia's command."

"It's true," said Quentin. "The fifteen knights in my unit saw it. They can attest to the whole thing. I doubt you'd believe that they *all* misunderstood what they saw."

"I see," said Cyril. "Zackary, your silly suggestion to continue this meeting over drinks is starting to sound appealing. I...don't think I can finish this talk without a hard drink." He shook his head and stared at the ceiling, drained. "Ha ha ha... Fia commanding the legendary, ancient black dragon? Hm. Perhaps...this is a tribulation from her."

"Tribulation? Oh, please!" Desmond rolled his eyes. "All right, so...Fia is in control of the black dragon. In that case, how do we use her? You said you succeeded in your mission, right? As in, you sent the black dragon back to its nest? So it's away from its master? Wouldn't that mean that Fia's lost control over it? How do we know the black dragon won't attack Fia now?"

Zackary nodded. "Good questions, all. Remember how I said there was a danger in you two knowing all this? Well, Fia's proof of pact is a single line with no breaks. In other words, the black dragon owes absolute obedience to Fia. It has a direct connection with her."

Desmond sighed. "Get on with it, would you?"

"This direct connection apparently lets the black dragon know what Fia is thinking and feeling, even over as great a distance as between Blackpeak Mountain and the Royal Castle. The problem here is that the black dragon, being the most powerful monster in existence, can think and make decisions independently. So if Fia were to, say, get angry at someone—to think for even a *second* a threatening thought—then the black dragon might just act on that thought by eliminating the source of her irritation."

"W-wait, you don't mean…" At last, Desmond understood the gravity of the situation.

"Correct. The black dragon can take action without Fia's explicit orders." Zackary bit back a wry smile and held up three fingers, bending them as he went. "Now, then—three reasons why this is a problem! First of all, the black dragon is absurdly strong. Second, the black dragon is abnormally fond of Fia, perhaps enough to cloud its judgment. Third, Fia hasn't explicitly said we can tell others about her familiar being the black dragon. Simply knowing this may put you on its hit list."

"W-wait, wait, wait, wait, *wait*!" Desmond stammered, flustered. "I know I said I was willing to risk my life as captain, but I didn't mean like this! I wouldn't have agreed if I knew it meant that my life depended on playing nice with the girl and her black dragon!"

"Nothing I can do about it." Zackary shrugged nonchalantly, clearly enjoying himself. "At least you get to be fake friends with one of the Three Great Beasts. That's gotta be worth risking your life for, right?"

"I-I-I'm definitely giving Fia a good scolding later!" Desmond shouted to no one in particular. "She needs to put some thought into who she befriends! Agh, what was she thinking, befriending the strongest monster on the continent?!"

Desmond homed his sights on Cyril—now *that* was someone he could vent his frustration on. "Cyril! This wouldn't have happened if you'd kept a tighter leash on Fia! Train your knights properly, at least to the point that they wouldn't think of making the strongest monster their familiar without consulting you! What does it say about you as a captain if Fia didn't even trust you enough to consult you beforehand?!" He was utterly oblivious about *when* Fia made her pact.

"Very well," said Cyril. "From here on out, I'll strive to become a reliable captain...someone Fia can confide in before she causes such problems. That is, after all, my oh-so-sacred duty as the captain of her brigade." Cyril smiled a little too pleasantly.

"R-right..." Desmond replied, nonplussed. "Well, as long as you kn—"

"So *you* had better fulfill your duty as well," Cyril cut in. "You should've known about Fia's familiar from the onset. Oh, and much of Zackary and Quentin's explanation is still nothing but conjecture. For now, we can't possibly tell the Commander a thing, so please test firsthand what parts of their explanation are and aren't speculation. Please and thank you, Commandant Desmond."

"Wh-what?!" Desmond exclaimed.

"You're a healthy man with a healthy body. Go use that body to do some tests," Cyril said. His smile was cold as ice, but Desmond could feel the fiery anger behind it all too clearly.

"W-wait, please! I was just venting! I'm sorry!" Desmond apologized profusely, but Cyril's chilly smile remained.

Gideon, who had been silent until then, stood up. He reached a trembling hand into his uniform and pulled out a letter. "C-C-Captain Cyril! I-I would like to step down from my position as vice-captain of the Fourth Monster Tamer Knight Brigade." The letter in his hand read *Notice of Resignation.*

"Wait, Gideon, what are you doing?! And...and aren't you supposed to hand those kinds of things to *me*?!" Quentin snapped.

"I'm aware, but...Captain, if I handed it to you, you'd probably tear it up. I-I've said some incredibly disrespectful things to Fia and her familiar! I-I-I never could've imagined that her little blue monster was really the Black Dragon King!"

"Well, Gideon," said Desmond calmly, "that goes for all of us."

"Indeed," added Cyril. "While her familiar's neck was strangely long for a Blue Dove, there was no way one would think it was the black dragon from that alone."

Gideon continued as if he hadn't heard them. "I'd have been killed by now if it wasn't for the kindness of Fia and the Black Dragon King!" he cried. "I'm ashamed to think that I never realized Fia's familiar was the Black Dragon King, even though Captain Quentin figured it out on his first meeting!"

The resignation letter crinkled in his hand as he looked at Cyril with pleading eyes.

"I..." Gideon swallowed dryly. "I had already intended to step down from my post for the unknightly things I did to Fia, but now I know that I've insulted the Black Dragon King and its master! Someone who couldn't recognize a monster as powerful as the Black Dragon King is not fit to be vice-captain of the Fourth Monster Tamer Knight Brigade!" Gideon bowed his head as low as he could, still holding his resignation letter in front of him.

"Interesting." Cyril sent a look Quentin's way. "Your thoughts?" Cyril knew that Quentin looked after his subordinates dearly, and he wanted to give him an opportunity to refute Gideon's words.

But, with a deep nod, Quentin did the opposite. "I understand Gideon's feelings on the matter. The vice-captain of the Fourth Monster Tamer Knight Brigade should either be learned in monster matters or step down."

Cyril looked surprised. "Quentin?"

Quentin's voice was dead serious. "I didn't have time to prepare a letter, but I feel the same way as Gideon does. Today's events have made it painfully clear that I do not have the knowledge required to be captain. I would like to step down and assume post as vice-captain instead."

Cyril went dead silent, a look of horror on his face as he realized where this was headed.

Desmond, on the other hand, didn't have a clue. "What the hell are you saying, Quentin?!" he roared. "There isn't anyone who knows more about monsters than you, nor anyone with a stronger familiar than you! Are you expecting us to just leave the captain position empty?!"

"D-Desmond, you idiot, don't!" Cyril blared.

"I recommend," Quentin proudly declared, "that Miss Fia take my position!"

Cyril glared silently.

Desmond gaped. "Huh?"

Zackary winced. "Are you mad?!"

"As I am making this statement before two other captains," Quentin said calmly, "this is to be considered an official endorsement. Today's events have made it clear that Fia has far more knowledge of monsters than I. Coupled with the fact that her familiar is the Black Dragon King, the continent's strongest monster, and her ability to command the familiars of others? I see no reason why she shouldn't be captain."

"No, no, no, wait just a minute!" Zackary exclaimed. "It takes much more than that to be a captain! And Fia's just a recruit! Think about it! She's far too...*lacking* in a variety of ways to be a captain!"

"That's why I will support her as vice-captain," said Quentin calmly. "Cyril, can you announce this at the next captain's meeting?"

The moment Quentin had asked, Cyril narrowed his eyes at the resignation letter in Gideon's hand and whispered something. A sudden gust of wind blew through the conference room, tearing the resignation letter into scraps.

"Huh? H-huh?!" Gideon watched the sudden updraft scatter the pieces of his resignation letter throughout the sealed room.

Coolly, as if nothing had happened, Cyril nodded. "Now, then...what were we talking about? Ah, yes. Quentin and Gideon said they felt they lacked the knowledge their position demanded and were going to devote themselves to further research and study. How forward-thinking of you."

The four men were at a loss for words in the face of Cyril's oh-so-gregarious smile.

"Cyril, y-you..." Desmond blustered. "I thought you weren't supposed to use magic outside of combat!"

"Do you have any proof I did?"

"Proof, man?" Desmond snapped. "We all saw you use wind magic just now!"

"Oh? So you *do* have proof?" Cyril kept smiling, feigning ignorance to the bitter end.

Desmond sighed. He then turned to Quentin. "Give it up. Cyril never budges when he gets like this. No matter how many letters of resignation you give him, he'll pretend it never happened."

"But—" Quentin started.

Desmond wouldn't let him finish. "Besides, there's no way Fia could be a captain. Even supposing she's more knowledgeable about monsters than you, she's lacking in little areas like common sense, reading between the lines...really, just staying out of trouble in general!" He jumped out of his chair and onto his feet. "Screw it! It's early, but Zackary's right! Let's drink!" His hands moved restlessly, first taking off his diagonal sash and then his uniform jacket. "I've worked enough today. *This* captain's done for the night!"

He waltzed out of the conference room, and Cyril followed shortly after. Quentin and Gideon figured there wasn't anything they could do but follow after them. Zackary came last, shutting the door behind them.

On their way to their high-end recreation room, the five knights saw something unsettling in the courtyard: a young girl letting out strange shrieks as she rolled in the grass—in fact, the very same young girl they were discussing moments prior.

"Hey, Cyril," said Zackary, "what's your knight doing over there playing in the grass, eh? Gonna do anything about it?"

"I would, but I do recall her being assigned to today's expedition," said Cyril. "Doesn't that put her under your command until the sun goes down?"

"Oh, how kind of you to lend us your knight for so long!" Zackary replied. "Unfortunately, *that* expedition ended before noon, so as much as I'd *hate* to say it, Fia's no longer under my jurisdiction." Meanwhile, Fia let out a shrill cry, extending a hand to the sky as she knelt on one knee.

"Hm." Desmond's curiosity got the better of him. "What are you doing, Fia?"

Fia looked surprised. "O-oh! What are you all doing *heeeeeere*?!"

"F-Fia?! Are you injured?!" Cyril asked. All five of them ran over at once, realizing she wasn't playing in the grass at all. She was writhing.

Fia held out her palm. "I hurt...I hurt my hand, so I drank a healing potion. But the paaaiiin!" They could see a light scratch on her palm, an injury that would've easily healed in a few days if she'd left it alone.

"I take it, Fia, that you're one of those who feel intense pain from drinking healing potions?" asked Cyril. "So why'd you drink one for a mere scratch?"

"I-I wanted to test the healing potions. I cut the effects short last time because it hurt too much, but I think I can go the distance this time...?"

"Cut short?" Cyril repeated. "You mean the healing potion's effects ran out last time? I thought your wound healed cleanly, though. Regardless, a scratch like that should heal with a single healing potion. For now, though, there's nothing you can do about the pain. Just do your best to bear it."

Fia nodded, unable to say anything through the pain. Worried, Cyril suggested they take her to the infirmary. The other four agreed.

"I'm fine!" she insisted. "Look, I'm already heaaaaa—*eeeaaak!*" She squealed as Cyril carried her.

"You seriously thought *she* should be a captain like us, Quentin?" Desmond said wearily.

"I still do," he replied. "She would have me supporting her as vice-captain. Every great captain leaves some work for their vice-captain, after all."

Desmond, Captain of the Second Knight Brigade

I THINK IT'S SAFE TO SAY it was the worst day of my life.

I'd just worked from one morning to the next, for a total of twenty-four straight hours—not an uncommon occurrence but surely an unwelcome one—but that was merely the beginning of it all.

Feeling my focus dim from fatigue, I decided I'd call it a day after I finished a few of my more important assignments, eventually doing so before noon. I was no more than a step out the door on my triumphant return home when a knight came running up to me.

Damn. If only I were a minute faster... I lamented from the bottom of my heart. Just one more minute and I would've been home free.

The knight informed me that Zackary was summoning me for a small meeting of captains. Meetings are never any fun as it is, but *small* meetings? Downright ominous. Small meetings are only ever called when there's top-secret information that can't be discussed openly at a more official meeting. In most cases, we'd have to take some form of action behind the scenes or carry a secret to the grave. This was an example of the latter.

The meeting was about how the black dragon was a familiar tied to Fia, a recruit of the First Knight Brigade, and how we would react to that fact.

Ha ha. Ha ha ha. Ha ha ha ha ha ha ha ha ha ha!

What could I do but laugh bitterly? Fia always, *always* caused problems some way or another, but she had truly outdone herself this time.

The black dragon was her familiar. Incredible! Absolutely, positively incredible! I wasn't sure whether to be angry or terrified. After our meeting, we moved to the officers' rec room to continue our discussion, but the topic was far too sobering for alcohol to do its work.

Ha ha...you're telling me that the black dragon hasn't reached adulthood yet, but it's already strong enough to overwhelm a blue dragon? Aren't blue dragons S-rank? Huh, two of them? Wait... what?! If something happens to Fia, the black dragon will die first? So the black dragon takes any damage inflicted on Fia? Oh...really, now? The black dragon can appear through a hole in space? Bah! Isn't that just dandy...

This is top secret, right? Who knows about it? Hmm...so the knights from today's expedition know some of it, but only us five know the whole story? Uh-huh...right. Too dangerous to tell the Commander? I see...

Oh really? A special task for me? You...want me to hint to Fia that I know about her relationship with the black dragon so we can collect information from her? Uh-huh...right, so the worst thing that can happen is the black dragon ripping a hole in space and appearing to silence me for knowing too much? Why are you running, eh?! Get back here and let me whack you real quick!

Huh...you're saying the black dragon, which is already the strongest monster of them all, will get even stronger by becoming a Dragon King who rules over the other dragons, and all for Fia's sake? Ha! You think I should maybe start calling her "Miss Fia" like Quentin from now on?

After that, Cyril declared he'd bring Fia back to the First Knight Brigade. Quentin and Gideon started complaining up a storm, but I was zoning out at that point. I was *done* talking about Fia.

I snatched a bottle from the counter, sat a distance away from everyone, and poured myself a drink. But I was still in the same room, and I could hear the four of them yammering on and on. Fia this, Fia that...

"Shut *up*!" I yelled at the top of my lungs.

"No," the four roared, "*you* shut up!"

We'd initially planned to lounge around until the feast, but time passed quickly. When we finally arrived at the canteen, things were well underway.

A certain young girl walked in through the door with Cyril, saving me the trouble of looking for her. She smiled as she parted with him before joining up with a particularly boisterous group of knights. Her cheeks were flushed, and she laughed freely with the knights.

So easygoing, I thought, exasperated but relieved. Fia was a rather impulsive sort, but she wasn't a bad person. Drink in hand, I approached her. "Hey, Fia! Have you tried the blue dragon meat yet?"

All the other knights cleared out the second they noticed me. I stopped next to her and gauged her expression. *What's with the long face?*

She seemed to turn glum the moment I mentioned blue dragon meat. Then she shook her head and blinked a few times, as if to try to clear her mind. "Of course I tried it! After all, it's the precious meat Zavilia worked so hard to kill."

"Zavilia? Who's that?" The name was unfamiliar. Maybe it was one of Zackary's or Quentin's knights?

"Hm? Um...one of my friends. He went home to Blackpeak Mountain earlier today."

"Mhg—*pffft*?!" I spat out my drink. "W-w-w-wait, wait, wait!" It couldn't be! "F-Fia, what?! N-no...did I just...say its name?!" I covered my mouth with my hands, wishing I could somehow undo what I said.

Fia looked at me with confusion as I continued to panic. "Huh? Oh, it's okay. Zavilia said he wants people to use his name because he went a long time without anyone using it. I'm sure he'd be happy to hear you using his name too... Wait, didn't Captain Quentin say something about this?" She hung her head in thought, clearly drunk.

Fia, you fool! If a little bit of alcohol is enough to make you utter such a taboo word, you should never drink again! "I'm dead! I'm totally dead! Somebody bring me a paper and pen! At least let me write my will before I die!"

This stupid girl! Everybody knew familiars didn't let anyone but their master call them by name! And this wasn't just any old familiar, but the legendary black dragon! A monster didn't rise to become one of the Three Great Beasts by sitting around doing nothing—it had certainly slaughtered enough monsters to earn that fame. Even children knew the Three Greats Beasts were bloodthirsty monsters, and yet this foolish girl had no awareness whatsoever of the danger her familiar posed!

"Hee hee, you're so funny, Captain Desmond! Zavilia might be super strong, but he's really a kind and gentle boy!"

My eyes shot wide open. Quentin had reprimanded me earlier for not understanding the power of the black dragon, but the one who *really* didn't understand was Fia!

I felt a hand on my shoulder, turned my head, and saw Cyril.

Cyril laughed. "It seems Fia is powerful enough to make the Black King pale in comparison! Either that, or the Black King hides its true self around her." He mockingly held out a pen. "Your pen, my friend. It was given to me by His Majesty the King himself. I'm sure you'll find it suitable for writing your last words."

"Blast it, is that your attitude when your colleague is in danger?! As Fia's direct superior, you should at least try to help!"

Cyril just shook his head as if nothing could be done. "But how could I ever hope to sway her? As you said, Fia didn't trust me enough to consult me about her familiar beforehand. Besides...

weren't you supposed to use that healthy body of yours to test some things? Investigate? Who am I to interrupt your work?"

"H-hey, I apologized for that already! Just how—" I began, but Cyril's icy smile made me think twice. "Just how, ah...good is that memory of yours, you wonderful mastermind?" I drew closer and flattered him.

I could complain about Cyril for days, but there was no denying he was the strongest knight in the whole brigade. As much as he frustrated me, he was the type to never abandon his fellow knight. I'd need him in case the black dragon actually showed up.

Cyril grinned like he saw straight through me and handed me a new drink, filled to the brim. "You look drunk, *Commandant*."

"Perhaps I am, *Captain* Cyril."

Oh, whatever... The knights were all safe after the black dragon mission, the alcohol was good, and I had these guys to liven things up. What more could I ask for?

I drank for some time with Fia and Cyril. It wasn't long until Zackary showed up to thank Fia. He exchanged a few words with her before looking satisfied and sitting down nearby to just listen. Quentin and Gideon appeared afterward, bringing whatever she wished for and singing her praises to all the Fourth Monster Tamer Knight Brigade knights present. Fia listened to the two prattle on for some time with a straight face but soon broke into a fit of laughter.

Things are peaceful. It was hard to believe we could take it easy and drink like this. I looked on as the captains gathered around Fia and, feeling content, took a sip from my glass.

It was a relief, really. Even if the black dragon appeared, some small part of me was sure that this lineup here could do something about it.

A Tale of the
Secret
Saint

Cyril, Captain of the First Knight Brigade

FOR PERHAPS the first time in my life, I, Cyril Sutherland, did not know how to handle a situation.

I had always believed that my world was bound by common sense. That belief had always shielded me...until today. Today, common sense seemed absent as strange, unbelievable truths revealed themselves one after another.

The feast was in full swing and the blue dragon meat was making the rounds when I arrived at the canteen. I looked around and breathed a sigh of relief when I quickly found the girl I was looking for. She was laughing away with that expressive face of hers, seemingly unchanged from when I last saw her at the captains' meeting the day before.

I imagined quite a few of the knights present here knew her true worth. Nobody dared to broach the subject today at our five-man meeting, but the black dragon was the guardian beast of the Náv Kingdom. If it got out that the black dragon was her familiar, the citizens would parade in the streets in celebration, and our stock as a country would shoot up greatly in the eyes of other nations. She could bring untold glory to our kingdom.

Now, though, she was laughing wildly, enough to make me curious what was going on. Watching her enjoy herself, I found myself smiling. Suddenly, she slipped away from the knights she was with. I wondered if she was going to get a new drink when instead she started for the door. Curious, I followed her outside and found her sitting on a bench in the courtyard, a vacant look on her face.

Please, have some awareness of your surroundings. Despite my best efforts, the knights of the brigade weren't all the virtuous, upright sort. It wouldn't be unimaginable for someone to try something uncouth, especially on a night of drunken revelry such as this. Sitting alone in the dark so far away from everyone was simply too reckless.

"Did you drink too much, Fia?" I'd intended words of warning but found myself speaking words of comfort. "I know that the night breeze feels nice, but you'll get cold if you stay out too long."

Fia looked up at me vacantly. "Captain Cyril..." she muttered. Then, perhaps because she was drunk, she stood up somewhat sluggishly and performed the knight salute. "I've returned from the expedition."

"Welcome back, Fia. I'm glad you've returned safely. Starting tomorrow, you'll be returning to the First Knight Brigade."

"Huh? Oh, uh...why was I in the Fourth Monster Tamer Knight Brigade again? Did I finish what I was supposed to do?" She hung her head in thought but didn't arrive at an answer. The alcohol must've been inhibiting her memory.

"Yes, you finished your task. You did well. I'm proud of you." Standing closer now, I looked down at her. She was small, only coming up to my chest, and she wore her heart on her sleeve. Yes, I had a hard time believing that a girl like her made the black dragon, a monster nobody could touch for a thousand years, her familiar.

Oblivious to my doubts, she began to speak. Her voice was miserable, uncharacteristically so. "Captain...have you ever had to part with a close friend?"

"A friend?" She'd caught me off guard. Who could she be talking about?

"I have this really cute, strong friend who flew someplace far away today to become a king. It made me sad, but it was what he wanted. I didn't stop him...but now I'm so worried about him. He's just a kid! What'll I do if he meets a strong monster and gets hurt again?"

Perhaps she meant to speak plainly, or perhaps she thought she was being vague, but it was clear she was talking about the black dragon. I looked down at her, shocked by her words. *Your... friend? Really? You're probably the only one in the world who can call the black dragon a friend.*

She didn't seem to be putting on airs as she called the continent's strongest monster her "friend" rather than her "familiar." The absurdity of it all finally made me understand. *She truly... might be the black dragon's master.*

Only then did I accept the truth. This small, young girl was a person of unparalleled power, or so I now believed. Or at least

I thought so. Looking at how sadly she hung her head, she didn't seem terrifying at all. On the contrary, I wanted to console her.

"In that case, could I become your friend in his place?" Maybe this would cheer her up.

She looked up at me in surprise. "Really?" She paused, staring at me as though trying to ascertain how honest I was. "Then... you'll talk to me? You'll go shopping and spend time with me when we're off work? You'll laugh and get angry with me and sometimes sleep on my belly?"

"There's, ah, a lot I can do there and a lot that I can't. That last one in particular seems like a bad idea, seeing as I'd probably crush you," I answered respectfully.

My answer seemed to disappoint her. Once again, she hung her head. "Right...nobody can replace him. That spot is his alone." Fia looked up and continued in a resolute voice. "Thank you for the offer, Captain Cyril, but I think I'll wait for him."

"Oh my. I've been turned down, it seems." To my surprise, I felt a pang of sadness in my heart. *It couldn't be... Did I actually want to become this young girl's friend?* Uncertainly, I continued. "What if you opened up another, separate spot for me?"

She thought for a moment. Then she smiled. "You're too kind. But if you become friends with your subordinates every time they get sad, then you'll have too many friends to count! You're already popular enough! Thank you, though. I feel better now, Captain."

"Ah, but...how am I supposed to get along with my subordinates if I can't be their friend?" I said with a troubled smile.

"Oh. You really want to be my friend?" She sounded like she wanted to console me. "But only equals can become friends, and you're *waaay* too talented and smart to be my equal!"

"Not at all! We're in an era of diversity. Our society will stagnate if we only interact with our so-called equals. The differences between us are just what we need to be friends."

Fia's brow furrowed. "Sounds...complicated. Can you...explain it in a different way?"

"You and I should be friends."

"Hmmmmm..." She tilted her head in an exaggerated manner, thinking.

Just one more push. "Fia, you are right in thinking my position comes with its limitations, but it also comes with its responsibilities. I handle almost all of these responsibilities alone, but there are times when I could use a second opinion. I'd appreciate it if you'd be my friend and help me in such times." Maybe my words were too hard for her to understand right now. I was about to elaborate further when she started nodding as if she understood.

"Ah, yep. That's one of the problems with being at the top."

"You...understand?" I couldn't help but ask. I thought that only people of my station could understand those worries.

"Hm? Oh, yes. People put a lot of weight on your words just because you're the captain of the First Knight Brigade, which means you have to be careful what you say. Can't really get advice from people easily either. It's kind of like how the Commander almost never gives his opinion on anything, even a simple 'good' or 'bad.'"

This girl was truly full of surprises. She often played the fool but always understood when it truly mattered.

"Yeah..." She nodded. "If the Commander's risqué personal information never got leaked, Captain Zackary would've never complained so much about his four-pack. *That's* why you need somebody you can confide in." Utter nonsense! The girl was wasted.

"Captain Cyril, am I drunk?" she added. "I'm starting to wanna be your friend too."

"Peculiar how *that* is what makes you realize you're drunk," I said, amused.

"Hmmmm, maybe you're the drunk one for wanting to be my friend? Okey dokey, Captain! Tomorrow, after we've sobered up, I'll still be your friend if you wanna."

"Really?"

She nodded.

"All right," I said.

"Captain Cyril, I was really lucky to be assigned to the First Knight Brigade. It's an honor to work under a knight as excellent as yourself!"

"Oh." Her sudden praise left me at a loss for words.

"Hee hee! I don't know why, Captain, but my chest feels all warm and tingly... Oh, wait! I know what you're supposed to say when you feel like this! I read it in a book a while ago. You say something like (*ahem!*) 'The moon is beautiful, isn't it?'"

Sure enough, above her flushed cheeks and beaming smile floated a dazzling moon.

Although I couldn't look into her mind, it was clear that Fia woefully misunderstood the loaded meaning behind that phrase. "The moon is beautiful, isn't it?" was a well-known phrase coined by a famous author, often used as a subtle and poetic romantic confession...but I doubted that Fia meant it that way.

"You're lucky that you said that to me. I'm probably the only one who understands your thoughts well enough to know that you don't mean what you're saying."

"Hwuh?"

"Ah, nothing. How are you feeling right now?"

"I'm feeling...happy!" She grinned toothily. "The shimmering moonlight makes me feel like all is right in the world, like everyone can live happily ever after!"

A little laugh escaped me. "You're always a happy one, aren't you?"

"Thanks to you, Captain Cyril!"

"Thank *you*, Fia. Now I'm happy too."

Something about her changed all the negative emotions I kept bottled up inside into happy, positive ones. The night wind was pleasant against my skin. In the distance, I heard the boisterous laughter of knights. Before me, I saw Fia smiling, and above her a gorgeous moon.

"Fia...the moon really is beautiful," I whispered in spite of myself.

A Tale of the
Secret
Saint

Melancholy in the Arteaga Empire

QUITE FRANKLY, the Arteaga imperial household was in dire straits.

The grand chamberlain's shouting echoed throughout the princes' joint office first thing in the morning, a common occurrence there. "Your Highnesses! What happened at the dinner party last night?! Did something about those noblewomen displease—*excuse me*, Your Highnesses?! Are you listening?!"

He complained in vain. The two princes, one green-haired and the other blue, kept their eyes shut. He did not enjoy shouting, but a grand chamberlain sometimes must.

"Yeah, yeah, we're listening. The ladies conspired against us last night. Said something like 'Oh! Those two princes are *so* terribly boorish. They aren't worth our attention,' and ignored us for *two whole hours*! Can you believe it?" The green-haired prince, the heir apparent, rolled his eyes theatrically.

"Your Highness!" the grand chamberlain said, aghast. "Please take this seriously! I believe I've told you many times that every lady sacrificed a great deal to attend that dinner party! I *also* believe I told you that, as the highest-ranking nobles in attendance, nobody would speak to you two unless spoken to first! Such are the rules of noble society!"

"Ohhh, yeah...you *did* say something like that." The green-haired prince crossed his arms and nodded deeply. The blue-haired prince to his side did the same.

The veins on the grand chamberlain's forehead bulged. "I simply cannot believe that you two could forgot such an important rule! How could you squander two hours with ten of the Empire's finest noblewomen?! All their attendants were in shock! Never has there been such a silent dinner party!"

"Yeah, totally. Quieter than a funeral, even. But what's wrong with that? So all the ladies were well mannered, eh? Isn't that good?"

"Prince Emerald!" he exclaimed, nearly shouting his lungs out.

The green-haired prince raised a hand. "The name's not Emerald. It's *Green* Emerald, got it?"

He grit his teeth. Their name change was one of the Empire's many problems.

It was well known throughout the Empire that these two, their older brother, and their sister—all children of the previous empress—had been cursed and lost the right to the throne. It was also well known that the three brothers then journeyed to a distant land to slay a powerful monster and rid themselves of their curses. But there wasn't a soul in the kingdom who didn't know the story of how they met the Goddess of Creation in that distant land and had their curses undone, returning to the empire with blood no longer streaming down their faces.

The three had always been ideal princes, in terms of bloodline and capability. Even in the past, many citizens assumed the oldest would be the next to succeed the throne once his curse was undone. But after ten—after even twenty—years of their curses continuing, the citizens gave up on them. Even the most influential nobles at the core of the government gave up when their close sources told them that the curses could never be undone.

Vying for the throne, the concubine of the previous emperor had a curse-maker work their dark magic upon the princes and princess...and then had that curse-maker killed. Under normal circumstances, a curse could only be undone by the one who cast it, although a *much* stronger curse-maker might do so. Worse yet, the death of a curse-maker only made curses stronger and harder to remove. The people assumed, then, that the siblings' curses were permanent. And so the empire as a whole had given up on the otherwise perfect princes...until their curses broke.

Prince Ruby, Prince Emerald, and Prince Sapphire—the three handsome, strong, brave princes named after gems removed their curses (well, two of them did to be precise) and returned home with newfound strength. The people of Arteaga had welcomed them with open arms. People love a good Cinderella story, and there was no Cinderella story as grand as theirs.

The three princes, the true legitimate heirs to the throne, had trumped their fate and returned to oust the previous emperor's concubine and her children from the imperial household. The citizens knew this to be just.

But it didn't end there. The princes' little sister—their Sleeping Beauty, if you will—awoke for the first time. She was a fragile yet pure-hearted girl, still ignorant of the world.

The citizens, their heartstrings all plucked by this fairy tale, gladly accepted Ruby as their new emperor, along with Emerald and Sapphire as first- and second-in-line princes. A new era had begun.

Which was, you know, fine. The grand chamberlain himself had wished for the change. The problem, however, was that even after quite some time had passed and things settled down, not a single one of the three showed any interest whatsoever in marrying—*nay*, in even engaging with the opposite sex!

This was greatly alarming in regard to the continuity of the imperial bloodline, as he often reminded the three. Whenever he did so, the three would (of course!) always apathetically reply, "The Goddess of Creation has given us a duty to fulfill. We have no time to waste on marriage."

The three instead spent their time worrying over how they had given the Goddess aliases rather than their true names, eventually changing their real names to correct their mistake. Ruby, the emperor, changed his name to *Red* Ruby, while the two princes changed their names from Emerald and Sapphire to *Green* Emerald and *Blue* Sapphire respectively. Why they chose to prioritize their aliases over their true names evaded him!

To be perfectly candid, he had no idea if the three had truly met the Goddess. He believed they did, though, for how else could their curses have been undone? He believed they'd met the Goddess, taking the form of a young girl. And he, as did many others, believed they'd never meet her again.

Meeting the Goddess had been a miracle, but miracles are miracles because they occur just once. There was no other recorded instance of a person ever meeting the Goddess. Her manifesting and protecting the imperial line could only be a one-time blessing. He wished that the three would understand this and turn their eyes toward the future, but...

"The Goddess called herself Fia! Isn't that a splendid name? So grand, yet so gentle and benevolent." Green Emerald looked spellbound as he sang the praises of a most common name.

Blue Sapphire had a similar twinkle in his eyes. "Her name is wonderful, yes, but let's not forget her sheer beauty. She had such wonderful crimson hair, like the Great Saint of legend, and though she was still a bit thin due to her young age, she had stamina great enough to walk the same distance we did!"

"Yes, she was amazing. A bit absentminded, but smart, gentle, kind..."

The two princes continued ad nauseam. Why had they been so silent at last night's dinner party? *This* was the problem! The two were so fascinated by the Goddess that other women weren't even on the table.

They were both young—Green Emerald being twenty-five and Blue Sapphire twenty-one—handsome, sociable princes, so of course they were incredibly popular among the noblewomen. But they didn't care.

Occasionally, between their long days of imperial duties and physical training, the grand chamberlain would overhear them talking about a woman—but when he listened in, he always discovered that it was yet another conversation about the Goddess.

It was a problem. It was a *huge* problem. But the biggest problem of all was—

"Green! Blue! There you are!" Dropping in unannounced was Red Ruby, the emperor himself.

The grand chamberlain hurriedly dropped to a knee as he strode in.

"Look! It took a while, but carefully washing the cloth Fia gave me to wipe my blood was worth it! It's almost white again!" he said, proudly holding up a cheap rag.

Green Emerald looked envious. Clutching his head, he said, "Red, that's amazing! I've been trying to clean my own cloth too—alone, of course, because I thought it'd be wrong to get another's help for a gift from Fia. But it just isn't going well."

Blue Sapphire slumped his shoulders sadly. "At least you *got* a cloth. I wish I'd been cursed to bleed like you two..."

Confounded to the core, he watched the trio express their adoration for the Goddess.

This was the biggest problem—their twenty-nine-year-old emperor was *also* obsessed with the Goddess, enough that he wasted his few spare moments chatting away with his brothers *about* her. The grand chamberlain couldn't even complain to him about his younger brothers' indifference toward women, as he was no better!

It very much reminded the grand chamberlain of the way baby chicks imprint on the first thing they see, assuming it to be their mother, and latch on to it. With all due respect to the princes, the three didn't have much in the way of interaction with the fairer sex during their youth. As a result, they became thoroughly smitten with the first woman they'd properly met, then grew obsessed with their memories of her. Worst of all was that the first woman they met just so happened to be the Goddess Herself. Of course all other women paled in comparison.

At this rate, the imperial lineage will come to an end. I must do something.

"Y-Your Majesty," he stammered. "Wh-why not perform an investigation in Náv for traces of the Goddess?"

This was the Goddess they were talking about. No matter how hard anybody searched, no such traces would appear—which was perfect. Once the search turned up empty-handed, they'd be forced to face the reality that their meeting with the Goddess was a once-in-a-lifetime event and move on.

Hopefully.

"Th-that's outrageous!" Red Ruby blustered hysterically. "H-how can you even suggest we do something so shameful as search for Fia?!" Despite his age, he was blushing like a tomato. Even children nowadays handled romance more gracefully than him.

The grand chamberlain kept his silence, exercising patience and waiting for one of the brothers to do his work for him.

Sure enough, Green Emerald also chimed in, equally hysterical. "Th-that's a bold thing to suggest! Looking for where she went, what foods she likes, what clothes she wears... N-no, we can't!"

I never said anything *about those last two—but no. Patience. Say nothing...*

Red Ruby laughed. "I don't need an investigation to know her favorite food! Meat, meat, and more meat! I remember her happily wolfing down all the monster meat on our journey. Wh-which means the two of us have the same favorite food!" he bragged.

"H-hey, I know that too! I'm the one who got to feed her meat and watch her up close, after all!" Even Blue Sapphire, the most well mannered of the brothers, was now a mess.

Ahhh... I wish the noblewomen could see this. The noblewomen saw these three as expressionless and cold-hearted, and had even taken to calling them "Ice Emperor" and "The Ice Princes" behind their backs—and who could blame them? They had tried everything, from batting their eyes to aggressively pressing their bodies against the brothers, but they were only ever met with cold glares. They thought the princes hated women. Of course, this was wrong. The reality of it was that the three were terribly inexperienced hopeless romantics who were unfortunately smitten with a goddess. It was up to the grand chamberlain to fix them...but how?

He was still thinking when Blue Sapphire, beet-red, spoke up. "I'll go to Náv! Yes, something this important can't be entrusted to anyone else! Let me handle it!"

"What? You sly dog, you! If you're going, so am I!" Green Emerald exclaimed at once.

"Guh, what?! Didn't we swear to rule the Empire together?! If my two brothers are going," Red Ruby declared, falling into the voice of a statesmen, "then I shall have to go too!"

Naturally, the grand chamberlain stepped in. "That's enough, all of you! Surely, you don't think you can travel freely as you did in the past?! Think of your position!"

Faced with logic, the three grimaced.

"Right," Red Ruby muttered. "In that case, we'll leave the investigation to Cesare. Any problems with that?"

Yes. Yes, there are many problems, he wanted to say. Cesare was the commander of Arteaga's Knight Brigade—he was somebody of great importance and certainly *not* one to send on a secret errand for the emperor. This was far too rash of a decision. But he supposed that these three believed that anything related to the Goddess took utmost priority and demanded no less than their best. Judging by their expressions, they weren't willing to compromise further.

The grand chamberlain put a hand to his forehead. His head was throbbing... "Ah. Understood. We'll...send Commander Cesare."

And thus, it was decided. The empire's esteemed commander was to go to Náv to secretly carry out what was practically an errand for the emperor.

It was early morning on the day of Cesare's departure. Despite it being a secret mission, Red Ruby personally went to see Cesare off, causing a crowd of people to form. To make matters worse,

Blue Sapphire was spotted among the knights in Cesare's unit, causing further pandemonium, the likes of which the grand chamberlain had never seen before.

For the time being, it seemed the melancholy in the Arteaga Empire would continue.

Fia, Zavilia, and the Hit List

TODAY WAS MY day off, so I lazed in bed past my normal waking hours, leaving the window open to let the breeze roll in.

This is the life. Why do people judge you for sleeping in when it feels so good? I wondered. But no matter how much I wanted to stay in bed, I couldn't stop my stomach from grumbling for lunch. Only then did I begrudgingly open my eyes just a smidge. The first thing I saw was Zavilia, writing away on a piece of paper.

That's a serious face he's got there. What's he doing?

Curious, I asked, "Whatcha doing, Zavilia?" Zavilia was surprisingly dexterous. You wouldn't expect dragon claws to write so well with a pen...

"Good morning, Fia. You sure slept well. I've heard that children who sleep well grow well. With how long you slept, I'll bet you grew some fifty centimeters."

"Oh, don't be silly—" I began as I got up, but stopped when I saw how much smaller than usual Zavilia was. "Huh? N-no way! I actually grew super tall?!"

Seeing me shout in glee, Zavilia nodded. **"Congratulations, Fia. I'd say you're around two meters tall now?"**

"Really?!" I grinned at the thought of being taller than Cyril and Zackary.

Eh heh heh! This time Zackary will be the one to ask me for help reaching a high shelf! Oh, I can't wait to see the looks on everyone's faces! That was when I noticed the ceiling was the same distance away as ever. *Hm? Shouldn't the ceiling be a little closer now?*

I looked down to see that the loungewear I went to sleep in was still the same length, stopping right around my knees. *Hmmm?! Did I only grow below the knees? My legs certainly don't look any longer...*

"You realized quicker than I expected," Zavilia whispered, voice calm.

I shot him an angry look, only to see him grow to his usual size. "Hwuh?"

"Hee hee, I thought I'd surprise you by making myself smaller than usual."

"Z-Zaviliaaaa!" I yelled, trembling with vexation. *Agh! I forgot he can change his body to whatever size he wants!*

He smiled and patted the spot next to him. **"Anyway, you were asking what I was doing, right? I was just working on my hit list."**

"Your *what*?!" That sounded terrifying! I leapt to Zavilia's side and looked at the paper he had been writing on, only to find a few familiar names...

HIT LIST

1. **GIDEON, FOURTH MONSTER TAMER KNIGHT BRIGADE VICE-CAPTAIN**
2. **ZACKARY, SIXTH KNIGHT BRIGADE CAPTAIN**
3. **CYRIL, FIRST KNIGHT BRIGADE CAPTAIN**

   •••

Yikes. My instincts told me this list was something bad. Very bad.

"U-uh, Zavilia? What's this for? It's not actually a *hit list*, right?" I asked fearfully.

"**No, it is,**" he said matter-of-factly. "**I had the brilliant idea of eliminating any potential threats to you before they could become problems.**"

"Whoa, whoa, whoa, whoa! What do you mean by *'eliminating'*?! None of these guys are threats at all! Especially the first one, Vice-Captain Gideon! He's as small-fry as they get!"

"**Are you sure about that? Somebody so deeply stupid and obtuse actually poses quite the risk. Besides, the weak ones are often the most unpredictable. For that reason alone, they should be eliminated as a precaution.**"

"Absolutely *not*! Rejected! Um, but...on the list, why's the second one Captain Zackary? What do you have against someone that brave and wonderful?" I quickly tried to change his focus to someone else.

"Wonderful?" he scoffed. "I don't care how drunk he was, there's nothing wonderful about stripping half-naked in front of that many women! He even made you count his abs, one by one!"

"Huh? Uh, I'm pretty sure he hasn't done anything like that."

"Right, right. You forget things when you're drunk. If you don't remember, then I suppose there wasn't much harm to you. It still irks me how overly chummy he acts with you, but you don't seem to remember that either. I suppose I can let him live. For now." I hadn't a clue what he was going on about, but it seemed he was letting Zackary off the hook.

I breathed a sigh of relief. "All right, then. Why's Captain Cyril third? He hasn't done a *single* thing wrong! He's an exemplary captain, and so kind and gentlemanly!"

"The fact that you can so easily lay three compliments on him like that is the problem. I'm your most loyal companion, and I do not appreciate others moving in on my position."

"You're cute, strong, smart, thoughtful, and always super helpful! There! Five compliments for you in one go! That's loads more than Cyril!" I said in one breath.

"All right. I suppose Cyril can live for now," he said, sounding unsatisfied. Still catching my breath, I peeked back at the list.

H-huh?! This list goes up to twenty! How am I supposed to finish this when I'm already winded from just three!

I gulped. "Z-Zavilia, why don't you hop in the bath? I'll wash your body for you and even dry you off after." He was fond of baths, so he took the bait as I'd expected.

"Really? Gladly. We'll continue this after the bath, then."

Agh! So he wasn't about to forget...b-but maybe if I make him comfortable enough, he'll fall asleep or even have a change of heart! I hoped to myself as I picked Zavilia up into my arms and carried him over to the bath.

A Tale of the Secret Saint

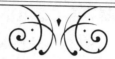

Fia's Scaly Gift for Captain Quentin

HMM... *Maybe there's someone who'd want this?* I pondered as I eyed the scale that had fallen off of Zavilia. It was bigger than an adult's head.

Every now and then, a scale would fall from Zavilia's body. Whenever one did, Zavilia's size-changing power would wear off and the scale would revert to its original size. I collected them as they came, and now I had a dozen or so, but I was running out of places to store them.

To be honest, they kinda got in the way. But I knew just the person to take them off my hands. I packed Zavilia's scales into a cloth bag and made my way to Quentin's office...

"Miss Fia! What an unexpected pleasure! Thank you for coming all this way just to see me! Of course, I'd have come to you if you asked!" Quentin bounded out of his chair the moment I stepped through the door. Gideon, standing by Quentin's side, looked equally ecstatic as he moved closer.

I sighed. *Jeez, is that any way for a captain and vice-captain to act? And in what world would a recruit ask a captain to visit them?!*

"Pardon my intrusion," I said. "Is now a good time, Captain Quentin?" But the two were already showing me to my seat. *I was kind of hoping to just drop off the scales and leave,* I thought, taking a step back.

But Quentin didn't read my body language, instead approaching with a broad smile. "Of course! I'd drop anything for you anytime, Miss Fia! Please, take a seat!" he gestured toward a sofa. I noticed the low table that Cyril had smashed some time ago was still split in two in front of the sofa—but wait, no, new legs had been attached to allow each split half to stand on its own.

"You fixed it by letting each half stand alone? That's...an interesting idea."

"Isn't it?" said Gideon proudly. "It's the table Cyril broke when I was insulting you. I wanted to keep it like this as a reminder of what I'd done."

"I see..." I looked to Quentin, the owner of the room, to see what he thought of the table. He didn't seem to care.

Instead, staring at me with intense interest, he asked, "What business brings you here today? Of course, you're always free to visit for any reason you want!"

His words reminded me what I came for. "Oh, right. I had some extra stuff, uh, show up? I thought you might want it." I handed him the cloth bag containing Zavilia's scales.

"This is quite a lot. Wasn't it hard to carry? What could it be, I wonder? Ha ha! Maybe vegetables from your very own home gar—" He opened the bag. At that moment, his jaw dropped and he froze in place.

"C-Captain Quentin?" His gaze moved up to meet mine, but he remained silent, mouth still wide open. "Um, Captain Quentin?" I asked again.

He blinked a few times, then pushed his hair back with a shaky hand. "M-Miss Fia?" He spoke so gingerly. "These sure look a lot like scales," he said gingerly.

"I should hope so," I said. "That's what they are."

"These sure look a lot like the Black Dragon King's scales," he replied.

"Yeah, I'd say so. They are."

"Ha. Uh. I'm sorry, this *might* just be my wishful thinking, but you wouldn't happen to be…giving me a few…of these scales? Would you?"

"No, I—"

"Oh, of course not!" he suddenly exclaimed. "There's no way I could receive something this valuable! Yes, thank you for bringing these in so I could admire their beau—"

"That's not it either! I was hoping you'd take them *all* off my hands, not just a few. If you want them, I mean." Didn't want to be too pushy, you know?

Quentin looked astonished. "All…of them?"

"Y-yes? Unless it's too much trou—" I was interrupted by Quentin flying off the sofa and dropping to his knees, then tightly grabbing my hand in both of his. "C-Captain Quentin? *O-ow, ouch, ouch,* my hand!"

"Thank you so very much, Miss Fia! From now on, I shall dedicate the entirety of my salary to you in order to pay for these scales!"

"Gwuaht?!" I blurted, surprised. "I-It's fine! I don't need your money! I was just sharing some stuff I had lying around!"

I pleaded that I didn't want his money over and over, but he was totally in a trance. I don't think a word reached him! He just kept clutching Zavilia's scales dearly.

Sure enough, on payday next month, he tried to give me a bag full of money. We argued for a while, drawing in a crowd of spectators. It created a weird rumor about us fighting over money...just one more thing on the long list of misunderstandings about us.

Cyril found out and summoned me for a good scolding. All I could do was pray that my sister wouldn't hear about all this...

Fia's Growing Pains Versus Zackary

I WAS HAVING TROUBLE reaching up to a shelf when Zackary happened to pass by.

"This, Fia?" He effortlessly grabbed what I needed, one-handed without even stretching.

Starry-eyed, I took the object into my arms. "Captain Zackary, you're so tall! Eh heh heh! Maybe I'll be as tall as you in another five years..."

"Huh?" he said doubtfully, as if he'd misheard.

"My father is a bit shorter than you, but they say children outgrow their parents, right? I'm sure I'll overtake my father someday!" I said cheerily.

"How old are you again?" Zackary asked, stone-faced.

"Fifteen! I haven't grown yet this year, but I grew a whole five centimeters last year!"

"I see. It's been five months since the start of the year, but you haven't grown a bit. In other words..."

"In other words, I'll grow all at once when the season's right, just like plants do in spring!"

"Listen carefully," he began. "While your two older brothers may be taller than Dolph, your older sister only comes up to his ears...although that's also fairly tall, isn't it? Bad example. What I'm trying to say is that you might be shorter than your father, just like your sister is, for the rest of your life."

His words were logical, but he didn't have the full story. As though revealing a closely held secret, I whispered, "Did you know that drinking milk makes you grow taller? My two brothers drank milk a lot, so they became really tall, but my sister hated milk. As for me? Heh...I drank more milk than my brothers *every* day! Even now, I still make sure to buy and drink milk without fail!"

"Uh, Fia—"

"That's why I'm *guaranteed* to grow taller than my father!"

Zackary's eyes went wide. He looked like he was about to say something for a moment but ultimately kept his mouth shut. He furrowed his brow afterward, deep in thought. "Ah!" he exclaimed suddenly. "Of course! Looking after her is Cyril's job! Who am I to overstep my bounds?" He slapped my back and laughed. "You just might grow taller than me one of these days. I'll be counting on *you* to reach things for me then, all right?"

I could see it now: me, growing two meters tall, looking down on little Zackary from above! It brought a smile to my face. "Hee hee! I'll be the one looking down on you then. Oh, but then I'd see your super-secret hidden bald spot!"

"Hm? My *what*?!"

"*Eek*, oh no! That's confidential information even by Military Police standards! P-please, don't tell anyone I said anything!" I pleaded.

"Wait, no, what are you even saying? If it's my bald spot, of course I wouldn't want to tell anyone! Who told you that bogus information? Was it Desmond? It was Desmond, wasn't it?! The bastard!"

"I-I won't tell you!" I still remembered Desmond's serious face then as he'd told me that he had top-secret information, moments before he keeled over in laughter and dropped that bomb. How could I have betrayed his trust?

I put what I was holding on the floor and covered my mouth with both hands so as not to let anything slip. I then remembered the proverb "The eyes betray more than the mouth," and shut my eyes.

Fortunately—or perhaps unfortunately—Desmond just so happened to be walking by and saw me, mouth covered and eyes shut...and right next to me was Zackary, who was shaking me by the shoulders.

Curious, he walked over to us. "What's up, Fia? Goodness, is Zackary assaulting you? Heh. I didn't know girls like you were his—*haugh*!"

At that moment, Zackary wrapped a beefy arm around his neck. "Hey there, Desmond. I hear you saw a bald spot somewhere on my head? Mind pointing out where exactly it was?!"

"*Ngh*... F-Fia, you idiot! Why'd you tell *him*, of all people?!"

"What?! No! I didn't tell him!" My eyes shot open at his false accusation, and I raised my fists in protest.

Zackary smiled cynically. "Hah! You gave yourself away, Desmond! So it *was* you!"

"H-how dare you trick *me*, the commandant of the Military Police!"

"And how dare the commandant of the Military Police spread lies!" Zackary bellowed.

"C'mon, it was just a joke! I wouldn't have said it if you were *actually* balding like, say, Cyril! I'm not that mean!" Desmond insisted, trying to lighten the mood at the expense of the absent Cyril, but—

"Did somebody say my name?" The air froze over. Cyril wore a thin smile, the chilliest and most hair-raising I'd seen from him yet. I didn't think for a moment he'd missed what Desmond said.

My mind was surprisingly calm as I formulated my next action—run away. *Sorry, Captains, but I'm not gonna stick around and get caught in the crossfire! I swear I'll come back to bury your remains...*

I apologized silently as I turned tail and ran. What happened afterward remains a mystery to me, because I never ended up going back to bury their remains (I was too chicken).

The next day, though, I saw Zackary walking with a slight limp and Desmond with bruises all over his face, so I got a sense of what happened. I saw Cyril later as well, his face and gait as pristine as ever, and swore to myself I would do whatever it took to stay on his good side.

That night, Cyril visited me to convey something or another while I was in the middle of my daily ritual—drinking milk. For some reason, however, he stayed at the door and stared in stunned silence at the cup of milk in my hands. I thought it strange but felt I might as well take the opportunity to curry favor with him, just in case a situation like the one yesterday with Desmond and Zackary happened again.

"Captain Cyril! I'll grow two meters tall super fast so I can be of more use to you!"

Cyril smiled, then wordlessly shut the door and left. *What was that all about?*

Whatever it was, I decided I'd drink an extra glass of milk that day. You never know.

A Tale of the
Secret
Saint

Fabian's Old School Friend—
The Shopping Trip

I T WAS A HOLIDAY, so Fabian and I went shopping in the capital.

We'd been friends for quite some time now, but he still continued to amaze me with how much of a gentleman he was. He always offered to hold my heavy things. Whenever we ate out, he somehow ended up paying for the more expensive restaurant visits while I paid for the cheap cafés (I suggested we take turns, since figuring out who ate what each time was so bothersome). Perhaps an heir to a marquess family was simply cut from different cloth than us common folk?

Such thoughts cropped up as I aimlessly shambled down the street, gawking at shops as I went. A decorative cloth store caught my eye. I'd recently gotten a new sword, but the scabbard was a bit too slick and could use something to give it grip. Some cloth would be perfect!

After looking through a ton of colors and designs, I purchased some cloth I liked. I continued through the streets with Fabian but bumped into someone—I'd been too absorbed in admiring my new cloth. Struggling to stay on my feet, I looked up and saw a vaguely familiar face.

"Well, if it isn't Fia Ruud. Walking with your eyes glued to your feet? Ha ha!" His arrogant laugh caused a distant memory to surface to my mind.

"We've met before, right? When the Knight Brigade admission exam results were announced. You went to the same knight school as Fabian. You were bragging about joining the Fifth Knight Brigade?"

Fabian let out a stifled laugh. "You have quite the memory, Fia. And after that, we got assigned to the First Knight Brigade! Harold here went pale as a ghost."

Oh, right. He was bragging that recruits who entered through the knight school graduate exam got promoted faster than those who entered through the general exam, but he was a real mess once he heard we two general exam passers were assigned to the most prestigious brigade.

Harold blushed red as a beet. "Th-that's all in the past! I've been making waves in the Fifth Knight Brigade since then! Captain Clarissa even remembers my name!"

"That's ama...zing?" I paused. "Um. Only so many knights join each year, so I don't think it'd be *that* hard for Captain Clarissa to remember the names of everybody in her brigade."

"Ha! At least try to hide your jealousy!" he snarled. "My name carries weight in the Fifth Knight Brigade, you know? They even asked *me* specifically to work today because they needed somebody reliable to protect the streets on this busy holiday."

I was speechless. It was obvious he'd been delegated to the work nobody else wanted to do—*working on a holiday!*—but I couldn't bear to tell him. Fabian couldn't either it seemed, as he remained silent and looked at Harold like a pitiable thing.

Unfortunately, Harold mistook our silence for awe. "Ha ha ha! Now do you understand my greatness?! Sheer luck might have gotten you into the First Knight Brigade, but you still don't have real talent like I do! Know your place!"

It's actually kinda refreshing how honest he is. Still, it's not worth the trouble to disagree with him. "Got it. I'll try my best to, uh...know my place!" *There we go! Nice and agreeable!*

"Ha ha ha ha ha ha!" he laughed. "Well, as long as you under—!" At that moment, a boisterous voice ran right over his words.

"Well, if it ain't Fia. What're you doing here, and with two hunks no less?" I turned around to see Desmond standing there, an exasperated look on his face. "Got a new man already, huh? Didn't Cyril, Quentin, and Zackary fight over you just recently? Was that not enough for you?"

"D-don't say that! They'll misunderstand!" I blurted.

For whatever reason—maybe he was busy?—Desmond just up and left without another word.

"Huh?" Harold began. "You're in the First Knight Brigade, right? H-how does Second Knight Brigade Captain Desmond know your name? That's the Tiger of Náv himself! One of the two pillars of our kingdom!"

"Huh? Uhh..." I hemmed and hawed. Should I tell him that Desmond and I were chess buddies? I didn't want to stir the pot or anything.

"Is that you, Fia? Out shopping?"

The moment I heard his clear, resounding voice, I thought, *Why, of all people, is* he *here?* From the corner of my eye, I saw Fabian sigh defeatedly. *Hey, I'm the one who's gotta deal with this!*

"Hello? Fia? Can you hear me?" the voice continued.

I had hoped he would continue walking by if I didn't turn around, but I was wrong—in fact, he did the exact opposite and brought his face extremely close to mine.

"Are you feeling ill?" Cyril asked calmly, pressing his forehead to mine. "I swear, you push yourself too far sometimes..."

"Wh-wha—?!" I stammered.

"Oh, forgive me. I'd use my hands to check your temperature, but I'm wearing gloves today." After confirming my temperature was normal, he backed away, looking relieved.

Harold stood to the side, lips flapping open and closed like a beached bass. "What? But...that's Captain Cyril, the Dragon of Náv! Both the Tiger and the Dragon just...what?" he muttered to himself, still oblivious to the real shock yet to come.

Hm? Oh, I see. Captain Cyril is escorting him, *huh?*

"What's that cloth for, Fia?" Now there was *another* guy standing in front of Cyril.

Fabian, astute as he was, noticed the man's presence even before he spoke and hastily took a step back to lower his head.

"Well, my scabbard's a bit slippery," I said, "so I was planning to wrap this cloth around it..."

The man—Saviz, the commander himself—nodded slightly. "Ah, yes. You were recently issued a new sword. In that case, I'll have a suitable cloth delivered to you soon."

"No, you don't need to—" I started.

"I was the one who issued you that sword, so let me send you a cloth that pairs well with the scabbard's design."

"Thank you...very much." It would be rude to refuse any further, so I took a deep bow and accepted the gift.

Saviz gave a slight nod and left. The whole event was apparently too much for Harold. He just stood there in shock with his mouth hanging open. I explained to him that Saviz only gave me a sword to make up for the magic sword I gave to the Kingdom after the entrance ceremony mock battle, but he didn't seem to hear.

After waiting five minutes for him to come back to his senses, I began to worry. "U-um, are you okay?"

His face was drained of color at this point. He gathered himself a little, at least, and muttered, "M-M-Miss Fia...forgive me."

"Huh?" I blurted.

He bowed once and then wordlessly ran off like a rabbit.

"It's your total victory, Fia," whispered Fabian with a smile.

A Tale of the
Secret
Saint

Commandant Desmond's Declaration Against Fia

O NE DAY, Desmond called for me after work. I couldn't imagine what he could possibly want with me, but I wasn't about to keep him waiting.

I quickly made for his office, knocked, and then opened the door to see Desmond sitting on a sofa surrounded by several of his subordinates. He was visibly on edge.

"Um, you called for me?" I asked.

"I did indeed, you *witch*," Desmond spat.

"Uh, what now?"

He angrily held up and shook some documents. "Enough is enough, Fia! Over half the complaints filed to the Military Police headquarters are about you! Why do you keep causing so many problems?"

"*Whaaat?!* That can't be! I always take my job super seriously!"

At that, he began dramatically flipping through the documents. I mean, *really* getting theatrical about it. Honestly, his memory was so good that you'd think he'd have all those documents memorized already. He was definitely putting on a show for me. But I'd play along if it made him happy.

"First off, this! An eyewitness report of you in the canteen eating lunch with Quentin, who *never* eats with women. He'd just returned from an expedition but only drank water, despite usually eating enough for five people. Correct so far?"

"Th-that? Um, yeah. I guess he did only have water, but why—" I answered, wondering why I was summoned for something so mundane when Desmond cut me off.

"I'm not done yet! It seems Quentin touched your left arm all over, after which you became offended and spat water on him... twice! Is this correct?"

"N-no! It's true he touched my arm, and it's true I spat water on him, but it wasn't because I was angry at him!" I had to clear my name!

He briefly glanced up at me before flipping to the next document. "There's more! On the morning of the black dragon search expedition, you had Quentin and Gideon all over you! Quentin was gripping your hand while Gideon was on one knee, begging. Anything to add?"

"Th-that's wrong! Captain Quentin *did* grip my hand and Vice-Captain Gideon *did* kneel, but they weren't begging or anything! Captain Quentin was praising me for something, and Vice-Captain Gideon was apologizing! That's it!"

"Uh-huh...so that haughty Gideon was on his knee apologizing to a recruit?" He laughed scornfully. "Sure he was."

"You don't believe me?!" I cried.

He flipped to the next document. "I saved the best for last! After the black dragon was successfully sent back to Blackpeak Mountain, you, Zackary, and Quentin separated from everybody to talk. From there, Zackary put you on his knees and hugged you while Quentin slipped away to give the two of you space...just what do you think you're doing in front of so many eyewitnesses?!"

"*Noooooo!* It's all a bunch of misunderstandings! Lies, all of it! I just had a hard time breathing, so Captain Zackary was helping me feel better!"

"I don't care *what* happened! I'm tired of half the reports we receive being this kind of worthless *crap*! Do you realize how much time I have to waste checking all this?!" Enraged, he threw the bundle of documents into the air, causing them to scatter around the room like cherry blossoms dancing in the wind. "You're really something else, Fia!" he shouted. "You're just so abso-*freaking*-lutely unpredictable! Ha ha ha! Hats off to ya!"

I watched him laugh maniacally. What was wrong with the guy? That was when one of the knights near him discreetly came close.

"Sorry, Fia," he whispered. "Captain Desmond had been working for two days straight when a fresh batch of meaningless documents concerning you came in. It was the straw that broke the camel's back. He'll be back to normal soon, and he'll probably apologize. For now, just bear with it."

"I...see. Understood," *Looks like everybody's got it rough,* I thought as I listened to Desmond's ramblings.

"From now on, I'm never, *never* bothering with any reports that concern you again! Got that?!" he yelled with a tone of finality.

"Yes, sir...oh. That means I have immunity from the Military Police, right?" I faked some enthusiasm. "Yay?"

"Huh? W-wait, really?" he fretted. "U-uh, Fia—"

"A knight never goes back on their word, right?" I interrupted. "Eh heh heh! On an unrelated note, there's this restaurant with really nice wine that opened up recently. If I drink enough, I *miiight* just forget everything that happened today...and I mean everything."

He went pale. "Y-you're not seriously asking for a bribe directly from the Commandant of the Military Police in his *own headquarters*, are you?!"

"What do you mean?" I deadpanned. "I was just saying my dinner plans aloud is all."

He grew quiet for some time. Finally, he spoke. "I'll do it... I mean, ah, please let me join you for dinner tonight." He began picking up the scattered documents, grumbling to himself. "Give me a break! I know you don't mean to, but you cause us captains so much grief."

Later on, Desmond apologized for his earlier behavior and treated me to a bunch of stuff at the restaurant. He was a nice guy after all!

He fell asleep sitting upright in his chair, likely exhausted from working two days straight. I decided the kind thing to do would be to let him sleep, so I finished my food and drink, then left without rousing him.

Unfortunately, somebody saw me and later submitted a greatly exaggerated eyewitness report to the Military Police, causing Desmond to summon me again the next day...

A Tale of the
Secret
Saint

Afterword

Hello, touya here. Thank you for reading this book. I'm glad we could meet in the afterword again.

This book expanded on Zavilia's past a lot and further introduced Quentin and Zackary to the story. I hope you enjoyed it as much as I did.

Depending on which store you bought this volume at in Japan, a different short story is included in the packaging. The problem with this, however, is that some stores are not readily accessible for some people. This gave me the idea to write a few short stories to be included with each book regardless: one about Zavilia, one about Quentin, and one about Zackary. I'm glad my editor accepted the idea, which I know couldn't have been easy, as the schedule was already moving forward by the time I started writing the short stories. Thank you very much!

Illustrations were drawn by chibi again. As you readers have no doubt observed, the illustrations are just as beautiful as last time. I'm sure chibi was very busy, so it means a lot to me that they took the time to draw them. What's more, my editor managed to get one more color illustration than we did for the first volume! Naturally, I was ecstatic. Now we just need a color illustration for Zavilia. One day...

I recently had my eyesight get worse for the first time ever. I've maintained 1.5 eyesight for all my life, all through preparing for entrance exams to my video game addiction phase and even through the time I was forced to work unreasonable overtime hours for days on end. I guess that's just how intensely I was working on this novel. I regret nothing.

I'd like to finish by thanking all the readers who've stuck with me.

To everyone who helped make this book a reality and to everyone who read this book—thank you so much. Thanks to you all, working on this book was somehow even more fun than the first.